CONTENTS

A LIFE WITHOUT SEASONS

There was a painfully loud noise when I flung the garage door open, like empty metal barrels rolling off the back of a truck. I could feel my spine quiver as I stood upright. It was one of those old heavy garage doors from the '50s that looked like it belonged on a barn in the middle of a Kansas wheat field. The racket I'd just made surprised me and I cowered, looking around to see if I'd drawn any attention to myself. I felt as though I were doing something criminal, partly because I was helping myself into someone else's home, but also because I had an unexpected nervousness fluttering in my stomach. Here I am, 27 years old, about to mow this woman's lawn. This wasn't some geriatric neighborhood widow, however. I wasn't getting paid in licorice and I wasn't going to leave with little pink calamine lotion spots on my leg for any poison ivy I might have had the pleasure of rubbing up against. No, I had other ideas of what I was hoping to rub up against.

My best friend, Georgie, works at a car wash on Sunset Boulevard. This same woman has been bringing her Jaguar in for the past few months. I'm always hanging around the wash, keeping Georgie company. One afternoon while he's soaping the woman's trunk, I manage to create some conversation. I tell her about the part-time office job that I have, "just to keep myself busy and my brain active, of course. I don't need the money." She tells me she is divorced and how her only kid has just gone off to college. This whole time I can see Georgie over her shoulder giving me the stink eye as he waxes her hood. Clearly he does not approve of my chatting up his sexiest customer. He and I have talked many times about how we fancy the "Jag Lady" and about how we'd love to be with someone quite older yet still very good looking like her. She's telling me about her house in the Valley and how hard it gets being alone so much. It's around this time that I decide to nominate myself for the job of mowing her lawn. Just for the exercise and to get out of the house, of course. I don't need the money.

It may only be 9:30 in the morning but this is L.A. in July and the sun is already trying to kill me. Inside the garage I see the famous Jaguar. It looks filthy. Georgie obviously sucks at washing cars. Granted, I am so hung over (or still drunk, I can't tell) that my perceptions are questionable. This is also the state in which Georgie tries to operate a hose and bucket every morning, so I can't be too hard on him. I focus on locating the lawn mower. I'm hoping for the riding type. No dice. Beyond the car near a door that leads into the house I see an old push mower that looks like the one I used at my parents' house the last time I attempted this chore fifteen years ago. There is a note taped to the handle that says something about her going to be out all day and there being bottled water stacked by a toolbox in the corner. I'm not in the mood to read and am now considering going home what with the loss of any potential of a porn-film-type scenario where my new employer appears at the front door wearing only panties and a silk cape, holding a pitcher of lemonade and beckoning me to join her inside for a well-deserved yard work break. However, realizing that leaving now would ruin my chances of ever coming to her house again, I decide to press on. The beastly mower starts up first yank. I steer it down the driveway, line it up, and get walking.

I'm dripping with sweat and am about to throw up from the gin burps and the pleasant Sunday morning heat stroke. I look behind me at the lawn. I've only managed six passes back and forth. Not even in straight lines. I made a neat looking Mohawk in the grass down by the sidewalk. I think my job here is done. This isn't worth it. Landscaping is probably the only thing this woman is ever going to want from me. I roll the heavy green machine back up to the garage and turn the motor off. As the engine noise fades away I still hear something running. I turn around and there's a Jeep in the driveway right behind me. I know this Jeep. That's Georgie's Jeep! Just then I see my lady come out of her front door. She was home this whole time? She looks incredible, too. Her long, doubtfully natural blonde hair is draped down over her certainly unnatural breasts. She's wearing an all-white linen skirt and top ensemble that highlights her glowing California skin. The sun does me a favor and reveals the silhouette of her lower half. She's the epitome of summer—a walking Beach Boys song. She looks like she's off for a polite game of tennis that requires no perspiration. She waves at me and says, "Good morning, honey" and hops into Georgie's Jeep. I can't believe what I'm seeing. He squints at me like he's an outlaw and they drive off. Now I'm definitely going to throw up.

Back home on the couch I'm enjoying one of several in a series of cold beers. I sure do like being home. Our apartment may be hot and small but it rarely fails to make me happy. The faded lime couch I'm sitting on has a lovely orange floral pattern dotted with cigarette burn holes. The floor's once purely tan carpet is covered in so many streaks and dark stains it almost looks to be an intentional design. Our kitchen features an old one-door Soviet fridge that functions so poorly we have to keep our beer (or anything else we want chilled) in the freezer section. Evening time has come and Hollywood's version of cooling off has begun to set in. I really like this time of day, especially on a Sunday. The entire building is hushed and the serenity makes me feel less guilty for drinking before dark and abandoning such laborious tasks as mowing the lawn. Besides, tomorrow is Monday and I've got to push 9 a.m. as far away as possible— that's when the whistle blows at my day job. Never mind that silliness now, that's over fourteen hours away. I can do a lot of very little in that amount of time.

I reach forward and grab a crumpled pack of cigarettes off the coffee table. One left. That's better than none. No sooner than I shake out the match do I hear someone shuffling up to the outside of my apartment door. I know its Kevin. Kevin lives down the hall. He has an odd speech impediment that causes him to sound like he has a perpetual cold, probably induced by his affinity for snorting powders. He says "v"s like "b"s and "n"s like "d"s, so we call him Kebin. To make matters worse his last name is Tonnis.

Kebin Toddis. Genius. Kebin is a large man with a fat red face who could turn me into a greasy spot very easily. His fist is the size of my whole head so I tend to let the jokes stop at his name. He wears his camouflage pants and flannel shirt with the sleeves ripped off every single day like a cartoon character. With his thick goatee and crew-cut Kebin appears more like someone you'd expect to find holding a shotgun to your head in Alabama than living in a pink stucco hacienda-style apartment complex in Southern California. Nevertheless, here he stands at my front door for the usual reason. I do have a beer in the freezer he can drink, but I'm out of smokes and he cut up lines of my few remaining Rolaids last week. Kebin also has the amusing habit of constantly referring to his dealer. Dealer of what drugs exactly I don't know nor care. At the time of this particular visit a song by Neil Young was playing on my radio. Kebin asks if I've heard the new Neil Young record. I oblige him and respond that I have not. Kebin says, "Yeah, I'be dot heard it either, but my dealer just got it and he says it fuckid rules." Great. Give my best to your dealer. The door shuts and that's the last I'll see of Kebin Toddis for, at most, a few hours.

As I'm putting out my cigarette and the song is coming to an end, I hear someone else out in the hallway. This time

I hear keys. The door opens and in walks Georgie. He strolls straight past me and into his bedroom as if I'm not even there. A couple of minutes later he emerges wearing his good jeans and his favorite shirt. He looks me in the eye and says, "Get up, we're going to Russell's." "You got butts?" I ask. He tosses me his pack and we walk out the door.

Russell's, as far as Georgie and I are concerned, is not only the greatest bar in the world—it's the only one. Russell's is supposed to be a sports bar but it's not. They have a couple of TVs and a plastic inflatable basketball with both the Lakers' logo and the Coors logo on it. That's about the extent of this bar's athletic pride. I've never seen a game of anything except quarters played at this place. To most people it's probably not a very nice place to visit. It's always dark inside. It stinks like a dirty ashtray and your shoes stick to the floor like they do at the movie theater. Despite this, Russell's somehow manages to hire the best looking girls in town who seem to be the most desperate for attention. Go team.

Almost everyone that comes here does so every day. Most are perched at the bar, just like you'd expect them to be. We, however, consider ourselves more dignified and prefer one of the tables—table 17 to be precise. Customers knowing the table number at an establishment may seem unusual, but we happen to be privy to all sorts of employee-only information. We're such frequent fixtures we could probably sit in on a staff meeting, if ever there were one. Confusingly, there are not even seventeen tables in here; ours is one of only ten. Good ol' 17 though is everything a bar table should be. It's high off the ground with two big black padded stools that swivel and have a backrest, and they've got that circular metal piece at the bottom for your feet. Sometimes I think we're more comfortable here than we are on our grimy couch at home. We've been coming to Russell's since it opened four years ago. The original lure was the Russell's "good neighbor card" that they sent out to apartment buildings in the same zip code for the bar's grand opening. This divine treasure gave its holder, and his or her companion, half-priced drinks. Any drinks, any time. Sadly, the good neighbor card had an expiration date of six months after it was issued. Their plan worked, though. That little passport to cheap blackouts had us back every single day. Despite the short run of the card and futile attempts to physically alter the expiration date of ours (as if they'd accidentally made one that was good for twenty years), the staff just continued the half-price hospitality indefinitely. I think they admired our winning attitudes. Four years later, we'd never think of going anywhere else.

We sit, light cigarettes, and order. I opt for a 7&7 while Georgie favors the rum and Coke. I'm probably just as curious about what Georgie was doing in the Jag lady's driveway this morning as he is about what I was doing there dry heaving with grass stains on my shoes. But, it never comes up.

It's difficult to keep track of time in Russell's. One obvious reason for this is our champion alcohol intake. Another reason (and a key defining factor in the greatness of any bar) is the stellar jukebox over near the bathroom door. Our appreciation of good quality music is unparalleled. Speaking of which, I decide it's time for a song and a piss. With an authoritative poke, I select "Manic Depression" and make for the toilet.

A strange thing about Russell's, regardless of its evident lack of class, is its baffling need to provide a bathroom attendant. I suppose they feel it necessary just because this is Hollywood, but all it really means is that it costs a dollar to relieve yourself. Not for Georgie and me, of course. We're privileged. We pee for free. There is only one attendant that works here. His name is Al. I figure he's homeless because he's here every day, seemingly every hour that the bar is open. He doesn't do anything but sit by the stall in a white collared shirt and black slacks with a little basket on his knee for money; it's not much different than begging on the sidewalk. Al claims to be a musician so he's always striking up conversation about random stuff while you're trying to go. There really is nothing quite like getting involved in a debate about Grand Funk Railroad with an oversized man sitting behind you as you've got your dick in your hand. I conclude that their albums with Terry Knight were much better before Todd Rundgren and Frank Zappa produced them, zip up, and head back to table 17. Upon my return I see that Georgie has moved us on to beers accompanied by much smaller glasses containing a clear substance I can only hope is tequila. As the hours pass, we don't say a whole lot to each other. Not because we're unhappy—quite the opposite. I've known Georgie for over ten years and we've never been much of the small talk sort. We sure do enjoy ourselves, though. I suppose some of things we do seem bizarre to others, but we have a good time. Often we'll drive all the way out to LAX just to drink at the bars. Airports are a great place to meet girls and folks of all types, coming and going from all points of the planet. We like to create stories about who we are and what fabulous destinations await our arrival. Escapism is a common theme in our friendship, I think. Sometimes we'll go to expensive shops like high-end furniture showrooms and converse loudly among the sales staff and snooty patrons. "Mmm…Georgie, this cow hide sofa would look striking right next to our giant pile of gold, don't you think?"

The glasses come and go in various sizes. Sometimes it feels like everything is happening faster than I can keep up with it while other times it's like we're drinking in slow motion. Instinctively, we both always know when it's time to leave. Often your body will tell you when it needs a break from the alcohol, or maybe we've just gotten bored. On some occasions it's obvious we need to go because one of us has fallen down or perhaps thrown something across the bar. This particular day I think we just want to go home because we're drunk.

An unfortunate thing about Los Angeles is the need to drive everywhere. Russell's isn't exactly far from our apartment but balls if we're walking. In keeping with upscale amenities like Al the washroom host, this wonderful relaxing getaway also offers valet parking. Usually when Georgie and I are at the bar we have an unspoken, ongoing drinking competition. Not for our bravado or anything stupid like that but just because we know that the more sober one at the end of the session is going to have to be the one to drive home. As we wait for the valet guy to bring out Georgie's Jeep I lean in and ask out of the side of my mouth, "Hey, you got this?" "Yeah," he says, "I'm cool." Indeed. Next thing I know, that little Jeep is flying down Hollywood Boulevard like a spaceship, dodging big trashcans on the side of the road as if they were asteroids. "Rainbow in the Dark" is coming out of the crappy stereo speakers so loud we can't help but sing along. I feel like we just ditched fifth period and are heading out to the old quarry because we heard some seniors left a half-full keg up there. Georgie manages to steer the craft rather efficiently, landing us at the right address. In a flash, we're on our couch. Noticing that the microwave is doing its job of telling time, I see it's 1:30 in the morning. I've still got a good amount of space to fill if I am going to maximize my evening before going into the office. I figure the later I stay up, the farther off work is. If I were to go to bed right now, my alarm clock would be squawking in my ear in what would seem like only minutes after my head hit the pillow. That's a terrible feeling. *Frampton Comes Alive* ought to do it. That's a nice long album that will get us through the next block of time. As the sounds of the crowd fade in and the band strikes up "Something's Happening," Georgie hands me a can of ice-cold satisfaction, lights my cigarette and then his own. All is well in apartment 121.

I woke up on the couch with a half-empty, warm beer tipped

over in my hand just enough to threaten spilling onto my leg. Oh no you don't. These are my work clothes. The microwave reads 8:15. Dammit. My mouth tastes like a dog shat in it while I was passed out and my head feels like Georgie hit it with a baseball bat. I get up and grab my keys. I see Georgie sitting on the floor leaned up against his bed.

As I slide into my poorly maintained yet fashionably beige Toyota Corolla, I can't help but laugh at the notion that I could get a DUI driving to work at 8:30 in the morning just as easily as Georgie could have last night navigating the spaceship home from Russell's. I take back what I said earlier. I should have gone to bed. *This* is a terrible feeling.

I sure do hate going to my job but I suppose I can't complain about it too much. I get paid a decent amount of money to not even have to think. I share an office with my boss who sits at a large mahogany desk to my right, while I work at a small folding table, Cratchit style. My boss is four times my body mass and has the calming demeanor of a psychiatrist. His bulging eyes are abnormally far apart and I imagine his thick spectacles must be an expensive custom job as they're designed to stretch all the way across his shark face. He's most hairy. The hair on his head was probably once completely coal black but a lot of gray has now grown in, causing a big white streak to run right over the middle of his scalp like a skunk's coat. His chest hair is impossible to miss because it jumps out of the opening of his collared shirt like a mess of rotten bean sprouts. He appears to have two separate beards, one for each chin, the lower being slightly fuzzier.

My boss hands me stacks of paper all day that I have to comb through for numbers that don't match up. The numbers are very tiny and I'm sure to be going blind. Thankfully my math skills are of no necessity; it's as simple as the numbers on the left matching the numbers on the right. If I find a 46 on the left and a 47 on the right, I circle them both and move on. There are eight columns of paired numbers per page. With all inconsistencies circled I hand the papers back to my boss and get started on the next pile. I must work quickly as a new pile gets bestowed upon me roughly every fifteen minutes. After three years I still have no idea what the numbers I'm examining signify. Thank goodness there is a bar a half block away. My boss undoubtedly thinks I have an intestinal problem because I leave our little office to "use the restroom" so often each day. By the time five o'clock arrives I'm about six cocktails in.

We have a radio in the office but, just like me, it's under the command of my boss. It stays constantly tuned to the local rock station. I know that doesn't sound so bad but the problem here is, like all rock stations across the country, this one only plays the same three songs over and over. I hate Supertramp, I hate Pink Floyd, and I cannot stand that Manfred Mann cover of "Blinded by the Light." Thank goodness I only come here on Mondays, Tuesdays, and Wednesdays.

The drive home from work is generally the same as the drive there. In the mornings I have to go over the hill to Burbank, battling the a.m. rush hour. Coming back into Hollywood at 6 p.m. is no easier. I spend the majority of what should be very little travel time sitting completely motionless in traffic. It takes me four cigarettes and nine oldies (plus ads) on KRTH both ways. Needless to say, I'm glad to be home. As I'm coming down the hallway I hear Georgie inside Kebin's apartment. I go in. The two of them are sitting at Kebin's kitchen table playing cards. Kebin is babbling on in his plugged-nose voice about some rare and endangered salamander in Africa that he most likely hallucinated the night before. I grab a beer out of Kebin's fridge, take a smoke out of his pack of "Widstods," and ask Georgie if he made it to the car wash today. "Not at all," he says. Kebin inquires what we're up to "todight" and Georgie and I stare at each other blankly. We tell him we're heading down the hall to our place to fix some supper. Twenty minutes later the two of us are at Russell's. 3,2,1, blastoff.

Thursday arrives. It's uncommonly raining and that's just enough to get Georgie out of going to work. Apparently the car wash doesn't do much business in the rain. Waking up at noon is a fine opportunity for starting this gray-skied day at the Chicken Place. I have no idea what the place's real name is. It looks like an actual chicken coop with decades old shingling sliding off the roof. It has the appearance of one of those hole-in-the-wall shacks you hear about on a dirt road in Georgia that serves up some of the best food in the country, except the food here sucks. It's just cheap and happens to be close to our apartment. Above the entrance hangs a weathered piece of plywood that features a cartoon chicken swinging a lasso. Inside, it smells like they mop the floors and wipe the tables with grease from the fryer. The menu on the wall is yellowed with age and offers two choices: fried chicken and fries or fried chicken and broccoli (for the health conscious). Georgie and I sit opposite each other, somberly eating. He has the unfortunate view of all the fat asses ordering at the counter, while I, over his shoulder, get the pleasing scenes of Sunset Boulevard outside. As I'm chewing a fry, I notice how our having lunch here is very similar to our sitting at table 17 together. I'm sometimes very aware of the satisfying companionship we provide one another. It's at that precise moment of stillness that through the window out on the street I see a monstrous 18-wheeler completely obliterate a small pick-up truck that was traveling in the other direction. I'm frozen. Georgie has absolutely no idea what I've just witnessed. The accident was so shocking that I don't even recall hearing a crash. I look at Georgie. He's staring down at his broccoli. I scan the rest of the place. Nobody is paying any attention whatsoever. The semi has long since blazed out of view. It all seemed to happen in a mere second. I swallow my fry, stand up, and throw the rest of my food away. All I can think of is that we pass Russell's on the way home. Maybe we can just pop in to see who's working the early shift.

We leave the Chicken Place. Georgie drives out the back way giving me no opportunity to see if the street on the other side has become a scene of flaming chaos and news cameras. He pulls into a drug store to get cigarettes. I jump out and tag along, pulling the hood of my sweatshirt up to block the rain.

I love drug stores. As Georgie waits in line I find myself hypnotized by the variety of items in just a single aisle. There are boxes of chocolates next to a rack of teen magazines. I see reading glasses for sale beside a selection of pipe tobaccos. I could pick up a home enema kit along with some lipstick without having to even turn around. And then I spot it. A metal canister filled with all types of walking canes. Immediately calling out to me is this very simple, dark cherry-colored, classic, all wood, old-man cane. I've got to have this. I should have a cane. Why can't I have a cane? $9.99? Oh, yes. I am having a cane. I sneak up behind Georgie at the counter and jab him in the back with it. "Ow, fuck. What are you doing with that thing?" "I'm gonna buy it," I snap, as if that weren't obvious. "What for?" "Well," I say, "aside from just looking cool, I think it might come in handy." He rolls his eyes and pays for the smokes. Walking back to the car, I'm practicing using my new cane like I have a bum leg or something. Maybe I'll tell girls that I had my knee blown off in the war. I've no idea what war. How about the war between the cane and my impulse buying problem? As we're driving back in the direction of our apartment I can see Russell's approaching. After a few blocks in silence I hear Georgie click on his turn signal and we both erupt with laughter. As if I thought we might pass it by.

I've not gotten but five feet inside the bar before I reach out the handle of the cane and fish-hook the waitress on her bicep as she tries to walk past me. "Give me a 7&7, shweetheart," I say, sounding more like Peter Brady than Bogart. She makes a face like she just swallowed a bug and walks off. I guess she's not working the tables today. Stepping further into the place I notice something different about Russell's. It's full of people. Seeing a good number of customers here is peculiar enough, but even more so on a Thursday afternoon. It certainly has nothing to do with "the big game" if there is one. Russell's TVs are never turned on. What an opportunity to test out the new cane. As we move in towards the crowd I begin to swing the cane back and forth in a sweeping motion, much like a blind man does with his walking stick. Instead of doing this on the ground at shoe level though, I am using the cane more like a machete, swinging it about waist-high as if I'm clearing a path for myself through the jungle. Expectedly I whack a number of people. For some reason I can't keep myself from saying "I'm sorry" or "excuse me" with each blow. It's obvious I'm hitting them on purpose. I think the cane serves us well. Making our way to the tables I can see that 17 is empty, with not even a glass on it. That's another one of the perks of having an allegiance to Russell's like ours. No matter how busy the bar gets, no one is allowed to sit at table 17 but us. It doesn't matter if we never even show up. It could be ten minutes after opening time or as late as last call and every single employee knows that this is our table and no one else's. Sometimes I'm amazed we get away with it. I can't imagine what kind of mayhem we'd have to incite to get thrown out. One New Year's Eve Georgie and I celebrated midnight by running around the bar slapping everyone's drinks out of their hands and spitting champagne in their faces. No one said a word to us—not one employee or even any of the people who'd just gotten a burning eye-full of holiday cheer.

Georgie orders a pint of cider. I have no idea why, but this makes me mad. He's never ordered cider. I don't say anything to him but I can't help thinking that now I've got to order something completely out of character, too. Fine. I tell the waitress to bring me a Southern Comfort and Mountain Dew. Two can play this game. Our drinks arrive. Mine tastes like Mrs. Butterworth's and Gatorade. I grab the cane and try to scoop Georgie's cider towards me. "Let me try yours." Before he can say "No," I've pulled his glass right across the table and onto the floor. The drink comes crashing down shooting shards of glass everywhere and dumping cider all over Georgie's leg. He gives me a disappointed look, like he's my dad and I missed catching the football he just threw to me. He sighs as he gets up and says, "Get me a beer, I'm gonna go put on the Stones." This is more like it. "Torn and Frayed." Nicely done. Sometime later our table is covered with so many empty glasses that it looks like we've been drinking with four other people. Around then, I happen to be gazing out the window. Maybe it's the long hours we've logged at the table, but I'm positive that the rain outside has turned into a light snow. Can it snow in July? The place had mostly cleared out. I think our time has come, too. As we walk outside I'm surprised to find that the sky is clear and it's fairly warm. I take note of the bright stars. Georgie hands me the valet ticket. I guess I'm the captain tonight since I spilled his stupid cider.

I'm awakened in the morning by the sound of Georgie slamming the front door as he leaves for the car wash. I glance over at my alarm clock. It's 10:43. Georgie's late. I have no trouble going back to sleep. The next time my eyes open it's because of the front door again. It's 12:20. Georgie walks into my room and announces, "They sent me home because I smelled like booze." "Did they fire you?" I ask. "Yeah, but it doesn't matter," he tells me with confidence, "I got a new job." This is a lot of information for me to process. "Get up," he says, "you have to see this."

I slide out of bed and into my jeans and then light up a half-smoked cigarette that is resting in the ashtray on my dresser. Georgie tells me to put on my shoes because, "We've gotta go outside." I find it a struggle getting down the stairs. Once I overcome the steps and make it to the curb, the sunlight's as blinding as angels. Spots begin to fade and shapes come into focus. I see Georgie in front of an enormously long, dark blue limousine. He has his arms stretched out with a proud smile on his face. All I can say is, "I don't get it." He informs me that he's now a limo driver. Apparently, after the firing, Georgie walked out of the car wash office and saw some guy getting a limousine cleaned up. Georgie casually asked if he was driving anyone famous. "Nah," the guy told him, "but last night I took the guitar player from Aerosmith to the Kings game." All it took was, "Boy, what a cool job!" The guy either felt sorry for Georgie or completely bought his gee-mister-what-a-swell-job-you-got act. Leaving his Jeep at the wash, Georgie drove his new boss back to the limo rental place and was then told to take the car for the day so he could get used to driving it. Georgie grins at me and asks with a bad English accent, "Where would you like to go this afternoon, sir?" We both start laughing as I get in the back.

We checked the limousine into the valet lot at Russell's. Inside was almost empty except for some guy at the jukebox and the red-haired bartender we generally referred to as The Rocker. We liked how she'd strut around and wiggle her ass in tight leather pants and sing along to the bar music. It was worth gritting your teeth through "Sweet Child O' Mine" one more time just to watch her hump a bottle of Kentucky Gentleman. I could see The Rocker already shifting her hips to the beat as she chewed on her pencil and did the day's crossword puzzle. As Georgie and I are enjoying our drinks at table 17, we're interrupted by an all too familiar voice. "Well, well, bitches. Come here often?" It turns out the guy at the jukebox was our friend Winky. I should've recognized him from behind by the knee-length chain wallet when we walked in. Winky is a good guy, but we've had to eject him from our apartment once or twice for hostile behavior. As Dylan Thomas supposedly put it, an alcoholic is someone you don't like who drinks as much as you do. Winky drinks like us but people handle alcohol in different ways. It's one reason that Georgie and I are able to be around each other so much—we tend to have the same reaction to nearly anything.

Winky has a real name. I think it's Warren. Regardless, we met him here at Russell's not long after it opened. He was a fellow good neighbor cardholder and we ended up seeing so much of one another that we became friends. I've always been fascinated by the way Winky speaks. No matter what he's saying, he says it with a tone of voice that sounds like he's just convinced a really great looking girl to go to bed with him. It's as if at all times he's got something going on that everyone else should be jealous of. I find it amusing to hear him talk to other people, but it can be irritating when he's addressing you personally. He sounds like he's trying to pick a fight even if he's only asking how you're doing.

Winky is on the shorter side in stature but impressive in appearance overall thanks to his unwavering cockiness and an innate resemblance to a young Steve McQueen. His facial hair is kept at that perfect state between scruff and a beard. He's muscular, and the tattoos on his arms look like the ones you only see on WWII vets—eagles, daggers, ladies' figures, Latin phrases and such, all done in blue ink.

As Winky stands before us at our table, Georgie and I sip our gin and tonics, listening to him breeze through speeches concerning his '65 Mustang, CCR, and pussy. "You fruits been down to Russell's Irvine yet?" Realizing he has asked us a direct question, I look at Georgie. We respond in unison, "What?" Winky proceeds to tell us about the new Russell's location that's opened about an hour south. "Yeah, I guess this place wants to branch out and cash in on frat boys." Makes sense. "What's it like?" I ask. "How should I know, it just opened last week," he says. The notion of a second Russell's is almost too much for me to get my mind around, but Georgie and I have the same sly look of wonderment on our faces as the possibilities settle in. Wow, all the greatness of Russell's but in a different town? That's like going on vacation while still having all your crap from home right there with you. "We should go check it out," Winky suggests, "see if we can't pick up some filthy UC Irvine girls."

Georgie suddenly shouts, "Go-carts!" After a brief pause for his bewildered audience he continues, "Family Fun Center is on the way to Irvine!" Family Fun Center is apparently an entertainment complex just off the freeway that has batting cages, video games, bumper boats, miniature golf, and the previously referenced go-carts. Winky reckons there'll be a bunch of single mothers there, too. "We could hit it on the way," says Georgie. What was starting to sound like a good idea reached the point of brilliance when I was reminded of the limousine parked outside.

It could not have been a more perfect day for a drive—the brightest and clearest Friday I've seen in my life. Breezing down the 5 in that limo seemed to me the single greatest thing we could possibly do. Georgie drove, with Winky and I stretched out in the back. We'd stopped at Ralph's on the way out and grabbed a few six packs. One of the numerous outstanding features of our new luxury auto was the miniature refrigerator included in the bar section. There was a complimentary bottle of champagne, surely intended for the next paying customer, complete with proper stemware. We managed to find in one of the cabinets a few airplane-portion sized nips of Jack, Captain Morgan's and Absolut, accompanied by four cans of warm Diet Coke. This vehicle was like our apartment on wheels but with more comfortable seating, a nicer kitchen, and about twice the legroom. The stereo was unbelievable, too—there must've been twenty speakers surrounding us. We were all three enjoying cold beers with the windows down and the sunroof opened up. Georgie's hair is a mass of wild, brown fuzz. He wears it long but usually ties it back to keep from scaring children and attracting birds looking to nest. This, however, was a special occasion and Georgie let his freak flag fly in the freeway wind. It flapped about with the fury of flames enveloping a mountainside; a glorious sight of raw nature. As all of these ingredients of our rolling party were coming together harmoniously, the moment peaked when "Feels Like the First Time" came on the radio. We yelled and smashed our beer cans together as Georgie turned the volume up full blast and pushed the gas pedal as far down as it would go.

Although we'd only been driving a short while, it seemed like hours—in a good way. I could tell that there was a unanimous feeling of wishing this trip would never end. It was like that movie *Stand by Me*, but without any real similarities. I think we all felt unified somehow, as though we'd just gotten away with a big heist. We were the coolest people in the world. Once we quieted down a bit and relaxed, this feeling of liberation, combined with a few beers and some bad mixed drinks served in champagne flutes, led to some emotional opening up. Nobody was confessing they were gay or telling how they'd once killed a puppy, but we were overcome with an urge to talk about ourselves. For as long as I've known Georgie I'd never heard the story about his first and only real girlfriend. I didn't know he'd ever had one. All I'd ever witnessed of Georgie's romantic side was the occasional Russell's waitress leaving our apartment in the morning. Not too long ago he was banging a small Mexican security guard for about three weeks. I thought that was his longest relationship. Georgie's story of his high school love, Cheyenne or Chablis or whatever the hell her name was, turned out to be a very boring story, but it was interesting to hear him share something personal, nonetheless.

We were talking about our families and our childhoods, different people we'd known over the years and what hopes we had for ourselves for the future. It was not unlike soldiers trapped in some hole together. We sounded like we should be saying our goodbyes to loved ones and promising that if we ever make it out alive we'll try to be better people. Don't get me wrong, we were still happy. We were just feeling a bit reflective, maybe. I decided to share with my brothers that I was thinking of becoming a poet. "I've been thinking about it for years," I told them. "The way I see it, if something causes you to take notice then it's something worth putting to words. No matter how meaningless or monumental it may seem, it deserves to be preserved with the words it pulls out of you." A dog crapping on the sidewalk, the color of some girl's lipstick, the steam from your shower, a hole in your sock, ice cream, the misery of working for your money, motels, leather, a new toothbrush, nausea, pizza, lighthouses, suicide, a full pack of cigarettes, the Grand Canyon, corruption in politics, the shine of an un-circulated dime, masturbation—if it has worth to you then it's worth putting to words. The words you choose will make up lines that no one else has ever written or read before. That's a power to be proud of.

Winky's contributions to the discussion may have been the most entertaining. Aside from a tale about the time he'd gone to a hypnotist to quit smoking and went too far under with a mean-spirited therapist and ended up farting every time he heard the word "banana," he divulged the history of his nickname. Something I was always curious about but never enough to bring it up in conversation. His story begins with him and four of his friends drunk on a Friday night seven years back. They'd gone out for a nice dinner and managed to drink far more than they ate. Falling out onto the street they begin their trek on foot looking for an establishment in which to continue the festivities. As they pass the Hyatt on Sunset they can see inside a formal affair that more than likely is offering open bar service. They may not exactly be dressed the part but are able to slide in and mingle easily enough. In a crowded conference room they notice a large photograph on an easel of a man posed with Howdy Doody. It seems they'd stumbled into an event for the International Ventriloquists' Association. Winky finds the bar. Leaning in, he yells out with his naturally condescending voice, "I'll have a vodka and soda with lime!" The bartender is elderly and professional and tells Winky that he's clearly had plenty to drink already. Winky removes his right shoe, takes off his sock putting it over his hand and says, in a drawn out, high-pitched juvenile tone, speaking through his crudely fashioned sock puppet, "Helloo there, I'm Mr. Winky. How's about making a drink for meee?" A security guard rounded up the quintet of idiots and pitched them out onto the street. Our friend was from then on stuck with the nickname Winky.

There it was, shining like a beacon of hope on the horizon— the giant, neon Family Fun Center sign. I imagine this is what the first glimpse of the Statue of Liberty must've looked like to immigrants sailing across the Atlantic to America. I hear a comforting, deep "pop" sound. Winky is slurping the foam out of the bottle of champagne as it overflows like lava from a volcano. He gives it to me. I tip it up nice and high and get a mouth full of bubbly that mostly forces its way down my chin and onto my shirt, then hand it off to Georgie. Winky advises us knowingly, "We gotta finish this thing off before we get out of the car, otherwise it'll go flat." That sounds reasonable enough. Taking the appropriate exit off the road, we pass the bottle of champagne around until it finally empties. As Georgie enters the massive Fun Center parking lot I am overcome with an emergency of the bladder. There is simply nowhere to park this thing and slowly circling the lot is making the situation worse. "Here, piss in this," Winky says, offering me the empty champagne bottle. I get down on my knees and pull out my cock, putting it right up against the mouth of the bottle. Once I get all lined up and ready for action, Georgie taps the breaks, pushing me face first into the barrier between the front and back seats. He and Winky are giggling like schoolgirls. Georgie promises not to do it again and, although I don't believe him, I have no time to spare. I form a nice tight seal between the head of my penis and the opening of the bottle and begin to relax. Unfortunately, the heat from my urine and the force it came out with created some sort of scientific reaction that caused the bottle to fire out of my hand and piss to go everywhere. The giggling turns to screams of terror. All at once I'm trying to control the explosion and wipe off my hands and get up off my knees, while Winky backs into the corner frightened and Georgie tries not to crash into another car. When we finally come to a stop in a loading zone area, the only place our vehicle would fit, Winky jumps out to make sure he didn't get sprayed while Georgie whips open the back door to assess the damage. "You jackass, I can't take this thing back smelling like piss!" I blame it on his earlier joke of hitting the brakes. Since he can't remember the timeline of events (it did all happen quickly), I manage to convince him that he's responsible for the catastrophe. Winky has already lost interest and is motioning to us from the entrance. "Hurry up!" he yells. "They have a fucking bar here!"

Inside was pure insanity. There were screaming kids

running in all directions with hot dogs and squirt guns and bad haircuts. I saw a mother pushing her fat child in a stroller. In the boy's left hand was a steak sandwich resting on his torso and in his other he clutched mom's Marlboro Light 100s. Nice. The bing-bong bells of pinball and arcade games were deafening, like the cacophony of slot machines at a casino, rattling off chimes of defeat for all to hear. Cutting through the fray we spot the modest bar that the complex offers for weary parents and adventurous passers-by like ourselves. It wasn't much, but in a place like this, an oasis for the needy is appreciated. Once we got significantly tanked at the Family Fun Tavern we were issued our own personal go-cart drivers licenses'. The whole visit was anti-climactic because no matter how drunk you are or how many times you sideswipe your friend in an attempt to make them roll their cars so they'll crash and burst into flames, those go-carts don't even go fast enough to thrill a toddler. Let down, we decided to have one more for the road and get back to the limo. Whilst finishing my gimlet I tried to persuade Georgie into letting me drive the rest of the way to Irvine. I've never driven a limo before and the pathetic laps around the go-cart track had put me in the mood for some real speed. There was only about twenty minutes left on our trip but I was still shocked when he handed me the keys. "Be careful, seriously," he cautioned me, "I don't want to screw up this job." I made sure to stop by the toilet on the way out.

Walking back towards the parking lot we were fairly disheartened from our pit stop but managed to focus on the real reason for this trip—the new Russell's. We were like kids on Christmas Eve wondering what glorious presents might await us in the morning. It was an exciting time in our small lives. As we approached the loading zone area where we'd abandoned the pissy limo, we all three stopped walking at the same time with perfect choreography. We noticed something was missing. The limousine. Gone. Nothing left but a curb painted yellow. "Shitfucker," Georgie says, "it's been towed." I guess I don't get to drive now. Getting back in the car with its monster stereo blaring and the sun shining was all I'd been thinking about. Oh well. Now we were in quite a situation: stuck at a Family Fun Center with no ride. "Our car is gone," I say, as if this is new information. Georgie gets a pensive look on his face. "Not *our* car, *their* car" he says. "Let that dick from Hollywood Limo Service come get it outta hock, I ain't paying for it." Good point. Not our car, not our responsibility, right? While Georgie and I were discussing the semantics of our grand larceny and how we were gonna get out of here, we realized Winky had disappeared. We looked around and spotted him over near a rusty dark green pick-up truck, talking to three young girls who fit in rather well in a parking lot. They wore lots of make-up and cutoff jean shorts. They were drinking cans of beer, smoking, and laughing horridly. They were fantastic— just our type. Georgie and I stroll over to catch Winky in the middle of some tale that he may or may not have invented involving himself and some Marines and a lawsuit that he won over the Nabisco Corporation. Georgie introduces us and the girls introduce themselves. I assume two of the girls are sisters because they look so much alike. They are both short and mousy with crazy hair. They remind me of Thing 1 and Thing 2 from *The Cat in the Hat*. The third girl, however, is a startling brunette who has my direct attention from the moment her mouth opens. "Brandy," she breathes from between her hot pink lips. Her outstretched empty hand gives me the idea that Brandy is her name. I put her soft fingers into my right hand and say nothing. I can hear Georgie explaining our vehicular disability to the group but I've still not let go of Brandy's fingers. I can't stop staring into her amethyst eyes—I'm transfixed by their warm purple color. I release my hold, smirk, and focus my attention to our predicament. Georgie is telling them about our pilgrimage to Russell's and it turns out that the other two girls go to UC Irvine. Winky has a look on his face as though he's just been reunited with his estranged dad. They've heard about the bar but haven't yet been. Who knows if they would've suggested it, but before they had a chance to offer, Winky said, "Well, load us up and let's party!"

Off we go like chickens in the back of their truck down into the promised land. Winky is in the front with Thing 2 and Thing 1 while Brandy and I serendipitously ride cargo with Georgie. I think this might even surpass the limo. We still have the wind in our hair but now there's female companionship, too. I turn and look through the back window to see Winky blabbing on. Hopefully he won't cross the line and get us dumped on the side of the road. Our friend has a special gift that allows him to sometimes choose the wrong words, especially with women. The speedometer indicates that we're traveling at a speed of 83 miles an hour. I look over at Georgie. He's got his eyes closed as the sun beats down on his face. Next to me is Brandy. I take a moment to study her. I look at her thin arms. Her skin is lightly dark with a luminous olive tone. She's wearing a tight white tank top with a black lace bra underneath that gives me no choice but to admire her full breasts packed in. When we met, I noticed she was only shorter than me by about an inch. She's wearing cheap brown flip-flops and I stare up and down her long bronze legs. I have to stop myself from reaching out to them. As I move up to see her face I catch site of her profile with its bigger-than-average nose. Brandy has thick long hair that's black and wavy. It shines over her and seems to illuminate her already glowing body. She's an Egyptian queen in a pick-up truck. I can't refrain from smiling as I watch her try to pull the hair out of her mouth in the wind and light a cigarette at the same time. I'm relatively sure that she is going to be the love of my life, at least for the next twelve hours. I can hear the dual guitar solo from "Ramblin' Man" coming out of the radio in the truck's cab.

We pull into Russell's Irvine. I see there's no valet service. We jump out of the truck and hustle towards the entrance. We've nearly forgotten our new mates as we blast through the front door, into the arms of a large man in a suit wearing black leather gloves. He grunts: "I.D." Georgie and I look at each other—doesn't he know who we are? Nevertheless, we show the man proper identification. Inside we find somewhere very unlike our beloved hometown Russell's. It smells good. It's clean. There are twice as many tables and they've got a full menu. I get a touch queasy when I realize that Steely Dan is playing on the jukebox. Bizarre. I find the closest waitress and ask if one of their tables is numbered 17. She points to one in the corner and says, "That one is, why?"

The table is big and round and it has six seats, occupied by six athletic young men. Georgie, Winky, and I approach. "Excuse me, gentlemen," Georgie says with respectful arrogance, "this is our table." The biggest of them stands up, resembling what an elk must look like standing on its hind legs, and says, "Is it?" "Exactly, that's correct," says Georgie. The elk says, "Well, we're the ones sitting here, so I guess this is *our* table." Georgie looks back at Winky and me. I give him a nod of confidence as he says, "Hey, I've got an idea. You see that street out there? If you get on it and start walking it'll take you right the hell out of my face." I'll admit to being a little worried for Georgie's face, but I'm not one to leave a friend in need. The other animals aren't paying attention to this impending altercation and they remain seated, mesmerized by a heap of onion rings. As Georgie and the elk stand eye to chest in a showdown of macho importance, Winky suddenly breaks the silence by diving in with some prison shank of a knife that I'm not surprised he owns, and lunges at the elk, landing the blade right at his groin. "Listen," he growls, "this is our fucking table. If you and your retard buddies don't evacuate now, I'm going to fix it so you never get to bang your ugly cousin again." The elk's face tightens up as if he assumes Winky won't go any farther, but a few more seconds on the receiving end of

Winky's unwavering glare and he knows he's dealing with a person who doesn't back down. The elk turns to the table and mumbles something. With that, his friends stand up and follow him off. "That was unbelievable!" I say to Winky. "Yeah, well, fuck 'em," he says, "Let's get some service over here!"

We sit down. Our ladies are at the bar with wide eyes. "Come on," I yell, motioning to Brandy. The three of them join us as a waitress comes over and asks what the commotion was about. "Nothing," says Winky, "those guys just suddenly realized they were late for something gay." We all laugh and order our drinks. I put my arm around Brandy. Less than impressed by the location, Georgie and I still seem to be enjoying ourselves. Had we boys come here on our own we'd most likely be having a lousy time, but the six of us made a nice group. Even Winky was making out ok. Good thing the limo got towed.

The mousy girls live together and we end up at their apartment. Thing 2 is in a recliner smoking a joint and Thing 1 is cutting up lines on the coffee table. Georgie and Winky are on their knees flipping through the records, applauding the titles they approve of and physically abusing the ones they don't. "Joni Mitchell?" Winky says, "No thank you," as he launches the album into the kitchen.

I'm on the couch with Brandy and scotch. We're talking about music and books and college (from which I dropped out years ago). She's an eager reader so I take this opportunity to force my favorite writers on her and tear apart the ones she likes. Humbled by my misinformed lecture she changes the subject to lost loves. Brandy dated some guy for six years and got her heart broken. I'm trying to understand how two people can be together that long while she's telling me what went wrong. "You were together six years, that's what went wrong," I say. She senses I'm bitter and that I don't really care about her story. "You want to go somewhere?" she says. I look over and see Georgie exhaling pot smoke and Winky throwing records. The apartment is right by a highway. Directly opposite the highway is a big graveyard. "I love this place at night," Brandy says, as we bounce across the badly lit, heavily trafficked road and down a mucky hill into the cemetery.

We set up camp on the final resting place of Bianca Ramirez. Born in 1899 and died in 1946, Bianca Ramirez was reportedly a loving mother and devout agrarian. Bless her. Under a black tree, Brandy and I lean back on our elbows and talk a bit. Her parents are significantly older than most parents of a girl her age. They're living out their senior years in Spain somewhere (which I consider a possible link to Brandy's golden skin) and I'm struck by the notion that her mother and father may still be in love. Brandy hasn't spoken to them in some time and she labeled her childhood as brief. As for me, I'm not sure my childhood is even over yet. I light up two cigarettes and hand one to Brandy and tell her how her eyes startled me when we first met. She said she knew. As she lay flat on her back, I'm propped up on my right side next to her. There's no stopping me. I flick my half-smoked butt over Bianca's feet and lean in for a kiss. Her breath smells like hot wine but when our lips touch I get a chill. My tongue enters her mouth and the tingly sweetness inside is unnerving. She squeezes me with surprising force, pushing her big soft tits into me. My hand runs up the top of her delicate thigh to meet the opening at the leg of her denim cutoffs. As we begin to kiss with intensity, I slide my hand up under the front of her shorts to her smooth abdomen. She's not wearing any panties. My hand glides slowly down. She's completely shaved. As I reach between her legs I feel something unexpected. My palm is rubbing up against what I recognize as a semi-hard penis. With our tongues inside each other's wet mouths, I grip her warm dick and it stiffens up. I begin to slightly move my hand up and down, just like I would with my own dick. She moans and then flips me onto my back and straddles me. Brandy opens her shorts and I see her erection. She pulls off my T-shirt, undoes my jeans, and grabs my pulsing hard-on. I'm beginning to really sweat— like steam is coming off of me. I can feel the cold grass and dirt on my back and I might melt through the ground into Bianca's grave. I take hold of her charged penis and we both stroke in time, she with my cock in her hand and me with her cock in mine. Brandy is breathing heavily, her hair hanging down near my face as we stare into each other's eyes. I jerk her off faster. Just as I'm about to come I feel Brandy shoot onto my stomach. I burst onto myself, mixing us together. As she bends forward and our lips meet softly, I wonder if this will ever in my life happen again.

I opened my eyes the next morning to find myself back across the road on the sofa with Brandy wrapped tightly in my arms. It was Saturday. I was happy. Brandy woke up and gave me a long kiss. She told me about a wedding she had to go to today and asked if I might escort her. I poked my head into one of the rooms and saw Winky on the bed, sleeping in only a shirt, with Thing 2 on the floor next to him fully dressed. When I went into the other bedroom I found no one there. I headed for the bathroom. As I was urinating I noticed a shadow behind the shower curtain. I pushed the soap-scummy curtain aside and saw Georgie passed out, naked, entwined with an also naked Thing 1. I rubbed some toothpaste on my teeth and tongue, rinsed, and chose to leave them be.

Brandy nabbed the truck keys off a hook by the front door and we hit a nearby diner for some breakfast. She whispered before taking a sip of coffee, "That was fun last night." All I could do was bob my head in agreement as the waiter put our food down in front of us. Once we finished eating, Brandy set out driving us to her place. She said she needed to get ready for the wedding. We were on the road for a while and I took note that the morning's bright sky was now murky and pale. There were threatening clouds above that gave me a feeling of unease and distrust for nature. We finally turned into the rocky driveway of a bewitching house on the edge of civilization. It was a monster wooden castle of a home that appeared to be two hundred years old with few updates since its construction. The house looked like it'd been uprooted from the shoreline of a New England fishing town and transported to this desolate spot on the opposite coast. Its exterior was probably once a rich brown color, but now sat dull and gray with its wood wind-worn and dirty. There was a long porch that wrapped around the left side and there were gables for the windows that lined the second story. It was cold when we got out of the truck and Brandy held my hand, leading me up a lengthy set of steps. I said, "You live here alone?" She just smiled. When we finally reached the enormous front door, Brandy heaved it open and ordered me to have a seat in the parlor. The only place to sit was at a piano on its rotting bench with dusty pink cushioning. The filthy black upright piano looked old and out of tune and had missing keys. After telling me, "Do not move, I'll be back soon enough," Brandy disappeared up a steep narrow staircase.

I had so many thoughts moving through my head and yet, at the same time, my mind felt clear. I just sat on that bench, soaking up my surroundings. The room was plastered with mauve wallpaper that showed white-silhouetted scenes of men with dogs, children playing, and women with parasols in big dresses chatting. Covering the floor was an immense faded Persian rug that looked depressed from living beneath the feet of people. I notice under the piano bench a pair of bright green lace thong panties. I pick them up and put them to my nose. They smell like Brandy. I tuck them into the back pocket of my jeans and continue surveying the room. On the wall in front of me was a massive mirror with a thick ornate gold frame. The mirror had a slimy looking film on it and gave no reflection of anything. It was hard not to get up and explore but my gut told me to stay put.

After a few minutes I must've dozed off.

I felt a soft touch on my cheek. Brandy was bent over with her face up close to mine. She smelled indescribably fresh and I was looking into those portals of eyes that have the most unreal control over me. She was wearing a crème-colored sundress that had a quilt-like floral pattern of red flowers, hummingbirds, green vine, and blueberries on it. I put my arm around her neck and pulled her the short distance to make our lips touch. I started sucking on her plump bottom lip and ran my hand up her left leg and under her dress. I squeezed the back of her thigh and she pushed away from me and stood up saying, "Mm, we don't have time for that." She tossed me a navy blue button-down shirt and instructed me to put it on so I would "hopefully fit in" at the wedding.

Back in the pick-up I got around to quizzing my date about the ceremony we were headed for. I learned that we were San Diego bound to witness Brandy's old girlfriend from her brief childhood get married. She hadn't seen this friend in years and said I could expect her to know no one in attendance. Obviously, everyone would be a stranger to me and me to them. I guess she felt the same about herself. That's why she wanted me to come with her. She said I was going to be the one there that she knew best, and also probably the one person there that knew her best. I had some serious apprehensions about traveling to San Diego when I thought about Georgie in the tub and Winky pantless. The guys were sure to be coming to their senses soon and I figured that one of the girls would be looking for their stolen truck. I didn't want to bring any of this up, though. I didn't want Brandy to think I regretted coming with her and I didn't want to jeopardize spending as much time with her as I could.

We arrived at an old stone building that looked to have been of some importance a century ago. Out front were carriages attached to ragged horses and there were long carpets rolled out for the guests. The sun had returned and the clouds dissipated. The heat swarmed around me as we walked towards the entrance. My armpits began to moisten with perspiration—I'd not showered in days. I took my lover by the hand and we started running, pretending we were on our way to exchange vows ourselves. At the top of marble steps, just through a modest foyer, was a massive ballroom. I gathered the ceremony and reception were the same event. There were ten glowing chandeliers hanging from the high ceiling and the walls were draped in red velvet. Hundreds of guests were dressed in long sparkling gowns and tuxedos with tails. Who were these people? I knew we two would not blend in well but didn't care and couldn't dwell on that for long. I knew we'd never see any of these people again. Brandy and I made straight for the bar. I was disappointed to find that only one beverage was being offered. I just wanted a can of cold beer. Out of a huge glass bowl a weedy old man in a top hat was ladling a tangerine colored drink into large chalices. I put my arm around Brandy and we knocked our goblets together. She gave me a wink and we both took a hefty gulp of the potion. There was a sensation more of smoke surging into my lungs than liquid slipping down my throat. I tasted pasty dust and could feel it congealing in my stomach. My veins were buzzing. I moved my heavy head to see Brandy at my left with a blank look on her face. I began to sweat again. "Baby, you ok?" I ask. She turns and hugs me tightly, burying her head into my neck, and starts to cry. "What is it?" I say. She looks at me with her iridescent eyes, shining with tears, "I don't know why I'm here and I don't know why I brought you."

Brandy is asleep with her head on my shoulder as I try to concentrate on the road. I'm driving the truck as fast as I can in what I hope is the right direction. The clock in the dashboard says it's 2:27 p.m. but it's turned dark as midnight and rain is coming down so heavily I'm just glad we're going anywhere. I don't want to have to disturb Brandy. I'm shaky and a bit dizzy with an aching head. If she feels at all like me I'd rather let her sleep. The air is filled with a fog, as though clouds from twenty thousand feet above have laid rest on the ground. The rain is now pounding onto the truck like baseballs dropping at a hundred miles an hour. There is almost no visibility and I can sense our little truck getting tossed in the wind and sliding around in the water amassing on the road. I know it's dangerous but I'm driving way too fast. I'm pushed with urgency, like something is chasing me. I begin to panic but can't slow down. I decide to wake Brandy. I need her to keep me from going through this alone. I raise my right shoulder up and down quickly two times. "Hey Brandy, I need you baby." No response. Slightly louder, my voice cracks, "Baby, wake up. I need help." Still nothing. I put my arm around her and begin to shake her. "Brandy!" I'm now yelling as I try to look at her and the road at the same time. I turn back towards her. I'm losing control. "BRANDY! BABY! WAKE UP, WE'RE IN TROUBLE!" Her head is just bouncing off my shoulder and I'm scared. Her hands are set motionless in her lap. Her knees are together with her feet wide apart. Every so often her head will nod forward and I think she's coming out of it. I realize I've been staring at her for too long. When I look back up and out the windshield there are two white headlights, twice the size of ours, speeding towards us. I had veered over into the other lane. Everything slowed to a near stop. I felt like I had an hour to swerve and get out of the way but I knew it was too late. I let go of the wheel and grabbed Brandy into my arms. I turned her face to mine so I could see those heavenly amethyst eyes. I wanted them to be the last thing I saw. Her eyes remained closed. I squeezed her lifeless body with all I had, and screamed her name one final time.

I feel swallowed by an orange glow. Am I alive? I think about my eyes. Are they open? Are they closed? I focus on the radiant color. It hurts. I'm looking through my eyelids. Concentrating on what I know should be a simple maneuver I persuade my eyelids to rise up. The orange glow turns to a blinding Christ-within, like magnesium set to a flame. It's the sun. My eyes instantly shut again. I think about my body. Can I feel everything? I'm here. Whole. That's a start. I lean forward and open my eyes once more. As I do this I realize I'm looking at the steering wheel of the pick-up truck. As if shot, my body jerks. I turn to my right. Brandy is slumped over in the passenger seat. Like me, she is miraculously in one piece except she shows no signs of life. Perhaps the clock on the dash stopped working. It reads 2:30 p.m. I throw my driver side door open and fall out onto the ground. In a frightened fit of teamwork my legs take control and force my body to stand. Our truck is unscratched and resting about twenty feet from the opposite side of the road, but facing in the same direction we were traveling. I remember the oncoming goliath. As I let go of the wheel in that moment of surrender, our truck must have slid clear off the road through the killer's path giving him free room to blow past. I wobble through the sloppy grass to Brandy's door. I fling it open and she remains motionless. With my right hand I push the hair out of her closed eyes and with my other I lift her chin to see her face. I kiss her lips. They are warm and she is breathing heavily. I shut the door and climb back into the driver's seat. I start up the vehicle and hit the accelerator but the wheels just spin in the wet muddy ground. Fuck. Our truck is stuck. Without hesitation I open my door again and grab Brandy by the waist. Sliding her limp body over to the driver's side I rest her heavy high-heeled shoe on the gas pedal. The weight of Brandy's immobile leg forces the pedal all the way down. The wheels again begin to spit pieces of ground into the air as the engine revs full on. With the knowledge that I'm the only one able to make anything in our favor happen right now, I move to the back of the truck and start pushing. Rocking the little truck back and forth I can feel it about to break loose. With a mighty heave of absolute desperation, I thrust my entire gut into the back bumper of that shitty pick-up. There it goes! I'm now faced with another dilemma. My half-dead new girlfriend is driving off in my only ride home. I scramble furiously after the recklessly moving truck as it slides around in almost a complete circle. Moments before it reaches the road I manage to hop in behind the wheel, hip-check Brandy back onto the other side, and reset our original course.

My keen Sacagawea sense of direction is proving useful. I know where I am now and remember the way back to Brandy's mansion. Driving calmly, despite my cadaver of a companion, I roll the window down and finally relax a bit. There's a pack of smokes on the floorboard. I try the radio but it doesn't work. By the time I flip the cigarette butt out the window I can see Brandy's big house and the dirty road leading to it. I make the left with a bit too much speed, throwing Brandy's head against the window. She rubs her forehead and lets out a soft moan. Finally. Pulling up to the house, I get out and scoop Brandy into my arms and carry her through the front door. Knowing I'll never make it upstairs with her, I prop her on the piano bench. With Brandy leaned up against the piano keys I finally get to look her in the eyes. "I need to go back for my friends," I say. "Stay here and rest and I'll be back as fast as I can." She puts her left arm up around my neck. I bend forward and kiss her mouth. She whispers in my ear, "I've always loved you." I'm overcome with the unfamiliar need to cry. I turn and walk out.

Approaching the apartment complex I can see Georgie and Winky in the parking lot and they appear to be arguing. Turning in I hear Winky shout, "There he is!" I pull the truck into the nearest empty space and Winky runs up to the window. "We've gotta get outta here." I barely have time to turn the motor off before Georgie drags me out onto my feet. The two begin to hurriedly escort me down the highway, one on either side of me like I'm Elvis being snuck out the back exit of a hotel. "Tell me what the hell is going on," I say. Georgie says, "Where did that shirt come from?" just as Winky says again, "We've gotta get outta here." I'm still wearing the navy blue button-down Brandy gave me. I lift my forearm to my face and smell the sleeve. She is here with me—my Egyptian queen. "We're in kind of a situation," says Georgie. "What? What happened?" I say. Winky looks over his shoulder and then turns to me, "After you left last night we stayed up partying with the girls. He's disappeared with one of them and I'm kissing the other one. Shitfaced.

I'm trying to get her pants off when she stops me and says, 'Wait.' She goes into her bedroom and comes back with a bunch of hundred dollar bills. She's got a thousand bucks in cash fanned out, rubbing it on her belly and shit. She goes, 'Let's have some *real* fun,' and grabs the phone and goes into the kitchen. I can't hear a word she says, but she comes back and goes, 'Can you wait a half hour?' We start making out more and then that's all I remember." Georgie says, "I wake up to Winky trying to pull me out of the bathtub. Both the girls are in comas. We're wondering where the fuck you are and then we see the cash sitting on the coffee table. Whoever that girl called last night either never showed up or couldn't get in because we were all passed out. Winky just scoops up the money and we split." I let out a long puff of a noise that could represent laughter, concern, or fatigue. "Well," Georgie says, "you can see why we're moving sort of quickly right now. She'll wake up any minute and find her money gone and I don't feel like meeting the crack pimp she sends after us." "What time is it?" I ask. "I've no idea," says Georgie, "maybe six."

Sometimes one does things to their body with such excess that life itself becomes difficult to recognize. It's maybe what having split personalities is like. You know that feeling when you tell someone a story and they tell you that you've already told them that same story twice? You genuinely are surprised and try to think when exactly you told them that story the first time. It's that same feeling but in every aspect of your daily and nightly lives. This evening I could really only be certain of the immediate present. I had no doubt that I was, right now, walking down a highway with Georgie and Winky in an unfamiliar town. I kept my mouth shut and centered my attention on the shuffling of my feet and the continuation of forward progress while remaining upright.

We couldn't have walked more than ten minutes before Georgie stopped us and announced that he had our problems solved. Pointing across the highway he said to Winky, "Get the cash ready." Following him over the road, I saw what Georgie had in mind. Surrounded by a hearse, a van, a go-cart, a washer and dryer, a birdbath, and a refrigerator, was a well-used Trans-Am Bandit (re-painted hot pink, no less) with $1,200 written on the windshield. This business we'd stumbled on was questionably legal. It also appeared to be run by a large brown dog chained to a tree. I won't lie, though—this car was awesome and it made me smile. A skinny man with a different kind of smile soon made us a foursome. "She's a beauty, eh?" We did not have time to bullshit. Georgie looked at the weird old guy and said, "If it's full of gas, we'll give you a thousand cash." We knew this was our savior. "Gentleman, enjoy the ride." The man took the bills from Winky, counted them, and then handed *me* a single key from his shirt pocket. We got into the car and, as I adjusted the driver's seat, I saw a tape sticking out of the cassette deck. I started the engine and it let out a thunderous rumble of relief as the exhaust released the machine from its rest. Pushing the tape into the stereo it clicked into motion the moment I put the stick into first gear. Pulling onto the highway, "City Boy Blues," the opening song on Mötley Crüe's *Theatre of Pain*, blew dust through the speakers and shook the dash. Picking up speed, the sun was beginning to set and I once again relished the gift of freedom.

It should now be less than an hour back to Los Angeles. The music is off and nobody's talking. I don't think I'm as eager to get back as my friends are. I had a much different experience on our voyage than they did. I feel different since meeting Brandy. I should have at least gone back to say goodbye. My pants begin to shrink every time I think about her. I roll my window down and follow the signs to L.A. Winky and Georgie are both asleep. I realize that tomorrow is Sunday. The weekend is not yet over. I consider turning the car around and going for Brandy. It's easier to just go on home. I don't feel right. What is it I'm expecting to happen? Do you know what it feels like to sense something leading you your whole life long? Maybe you can't identify it, but you, yourself, lead nothing and are pulled constantly by something unknown, that somehow your body tells you that you want. We approach Hollywood. Georgie wakes up and says, "Where are we?" "Almost there," I say. He turns around and smacks Winky on the leg, "Wake up, douche." Winky opens his eyes, looks out the window and says, "We're still driving? Jesus, are you doing 40?" "Look, it's our exit," I tell him. Turning onto Sunset Boulevard we can see the car wash where Georgie used to work. Parked in front, freshly washed and waxed, is Georgie's Jeep. "Hey, let me get my wheels," he says. I pull into the car wash and align the Trans Am with the blue Wrangler. Georgie hops out and Winky follows from the backseat. Leaning in through the passenger side window Winky says, "I'm riding with him. See you at Russell's."

I watch the two pull out and drive off down Sunset. It occurs to me, alone with the car, that I can go anywhere I please. Maybe I should drive back down to Brandy after all. I could stay there and live with her forever. I could fix her pork chops while she played the piano. I could mow her ferocious lawn while she read Dickens on the porch. We would laugh about the job I used to go to and laugh about how she used to live alone. We could never have kids. We would raise each other instead. We'd drink wine in the morning, make love on the hood of my pink Trans Am, and then play badminton naked in the back yard. We would be a living dream with a soundtrack that we'd create. One like no one has ever heard and one that no one else would ever hear. Songs as long and as short as life itself. Brandy's warm plum eyes would be the last thing I saw every night before falling asleep. I imagined a love with seasons.

As the fantasies clamber in my brain, I remember my friends. Though I have little interest in playing badminton with Georgie, he has been the most important fixture in my life so far. I decide to go to Russell's. Lodging the gears into reverse I back out of the car wash and turn down Sunset. I'm nearing the bar and my mind is still on the move. I envision a swarm of fire trucks and rescue vehicles surrounding Russell's when I arrive. The place is fiercely ablaze, entirely consumed in flames, giving off mile-high smoke signals that tell me to drive on. Georgie's Jeep is pulled off to the side of the road. He has his head in his hands sobbing as Winky gives him a consoling rub of the shoulder.

Rounding the curve I see Russell's standing just as it did last week. Telling the valet guy to take it easy with my baby, I let him get behind the wheel of the Trans Am and drive it away. Stepping into the bar for what seems like the first time in years, I move towards table 17 to join Georgie and Winky and their already empty glasses. "Another round, gents," I command, reaching for an extra stool. I believe this is the only time that anyone other than Georgie and myself has sat at Table 17. I go to the bathroom. Adding to my feelings of disorientation is the absence of Al with his basket on his knee, begging for money. I've never been in here without Al right behind me. I'm unable to piss in the silence. I pull out the green panties from my jeans pocket. I take off my pants and throw my boxers in the trash. I smell Brandy's underwear a few times and they take me to her. I slide them on, up my legs and over my dick and balls. I can feel the smooth thong settle in between my ass cheeks. I put my tight jeans back on over Brandy's underwear and leave the bathroom. I see Winky and Georgie laughing. They're drinking their beers and I can see mine, full and waiting. I walk over and tell the guys that I left my cigarettes in the car. They make no acknowledgement of this and I turn and walk away. I may not know what it is leading me, but I know that with discoveries come answers.

I hand the attendant my ticket for the pink Trans Am. I light up a cigarette from my pocket and await the arrival of my car. Standing there alone in the starry dark of Saturday night I smile. Tomorrow is Sunday. From now on, every day will be like Sunday. I don't care much for Morrissey but I like the sentiment. I have always said that my assessment of life—a summation, if you will—is that spiders can crawl all over your face while you sleep in your bed and you'd never know it. While this may be true, I suppose I can't spend my entire life afraid of spiders and I know I certainly cannot stay awake forever.

VENUS SPINS THE OTHER WAY

Like wasps flying for their lives, that damn hum started up at 4 p.m. every day. The local boys circled the hills behind the houses, running their snowmobiles full blast around Ring Road. I remember that December well. I was in Vermont with Barbara Jennifer. Jill was in Massachusetts loaded with cancer. Barbara Jennifer was nice enough. She insisted she be called by her two first names at all times. I'd find myself having to say, Barbara Jennifer is coming up for New Year's. Barbara Jennifer hates figs. Barbara Jennifer is being audited, and so on. Even her last name was a first name: Susan. Barbara Jennifer Susan. She was only staying with me for New Year's. I'd invited her. Her mouth didn't open much when she spoke. Her upper lip seemed to barely move, as if unaware that words were sliding out right under it. The lake was frozen that winter. People would often fish on the lake in the warmer months.

Jill had been on my mind ever since I heard she was sick. I really only knew her as well as I knew Barbara Jennifer, but I felt close to Jill knowing she was suffering. I felt guilty being in Vermont with Barbara Jennifer while Jill was dying in a hospital. I remember wishing that Jill could have been with me for the New Year instead of Barbara Jennifer. I wanted to get to know Jill more. I wanted another night with her. Maybe only because I knew she'd soon be gone. Maybe she wanted someone to know her better before she left. I'd never known anyone that I'd fucked to die.

That New Year's there was a snowstorm. On top of that we ran out of propane. We were on a mountain north of Bennington. The guys couldn't get up the road because of the weather until the next day to refill the tank. So, we had no heat. The local boys were shooting off fireworks out over the lake. Barbara Jennifer and I watched some bursts through the window. Golden sparkles blossomed with a bang, warmed our eyes, then quickly faded and fell toward the dark ice. It was before midnight but we decided to get into bed because we were cold.

I began to fall asleep right away. Just before I did, Barbara Jennifer threw back the blankets and said she was going for a hot bath. She was still cold. The water heater was electric. The empty propane tank didn't affect the hot water in the house. I turned over and was soon asleep. Later I woke, sweaty. Jill had died. I knew it. Barbara Jennifer wasn't in bed. I pushed off the covers and rolled onto my back. I tried to make out anything in the darkness. It was so dark I couldn't tell if my eyes were open or closed.

When I woke next it was sunny out and I was wrapped up in the blankets. Barbara Jennifer was still gone, or gone again. I wanted to tell her that someone I knew had died. I wanted to call every hospital in Boston. I had to pee. When I opened the bathroom door I found the bathtub filled with water. I put my fingertips in and felt the water was cold. I sat down on the toilet to pee. I didn't flush.

I went downstairs and saw just how much snow we'd gotten. Through the window I could see Barbara Jennifer standing by the lake. Wind was blowing snow around her like a fog. She was looking down and it looked like she was smiling. I called the propane guys to find out when we could expect them. They said tomorrow. It was New Year's Day after all, and a Sunday. I needed coffee. I filled the kettle with water and set it on the stove. I lit a match and turned on the burner. Nothing.

THE GOD BOX

I've been carrying around a lot of guilt for a lot of time. If no one ever reads this, that's fine. But I have no one to talk to and I need to get this out. All I can think to do is write it down.

I'd written that much when I thought I heard a knock at my door. I waited to hear it again to be sure it was real. Peeling back the curtain in my bedroom window I could see two clean young men standing at my doorstep. They looked much more alert than I did at 8 a.m. I wanted to know why and I wanted to know what they wanted.

"Morning," I said.

"Good morning, Sir," said the shorter of the two. "May I ask you a question?"

"You just did," I said. "What's the next one?"

"Let me ask you this, do you have an idea of how the world will end?"

"I have an idea. No one really knows though now do they?"

"Do you think you will be going to heaven?"

"Sure, if it's there. Wouldn't we all get to go?"

"No, I do not believe so. My friend and I would like to talk to you about your salvation."

"My salivation?"

The taller one grinned and I saw he had a gold tooth in the front. I thought it looked cool.

"Would you like to come in? I can make some coffee," I said.

"We would like to talk to you about your salvation. The coffee is not necessary," the shorter one said.

They stepped in. I said to please have a seat. They bent the creases in their navy blue trousers to sit on my couch, their backs stiff with good posture. The taller one smoothed his tie. Their ties matched their pants. Their shirts matched the sky.

"You're sure no coffee?" I said.

"No, thank you."

"How 'bout a beer?"

"No, thank you," said the shorter one with a quizzical look on his face.

"You?" I said to the taller one. He closed his eyes

and shook his head. I sat down in a chair, on the other side of the coffee table, opposite the couch.

"So, tell me then what it is you're after," I said.

"We are concerned about your eternal happiness," the shorter one said.

"So you're after me? Why should you be concerned about my happiness? Do you sense sadness in my future?"

"It is not so much your future we are concerned with as it is your post-future—your time after your time here on Earth."

"God, it's hard enough getting through life on this planet, you're telling me there is more I should be worried about?"

"That is just it—we do not want you to have to be worried for yourself."

"What is it you gentlemen are proposing?"

"I would not call our intentions a proposal. Sir, let me ask you, have you ever talked to God?"

"Well, I believe I've talked to *a* god. Is it *the* God? I don't know. Sometimes I think there are several gods, y'know? Like, more than one god."

"We assure you there is only one God. And it is *the* God. You would know if you had spoken to God. It sounds as though you have not."

"Well, my gods seem to fall somewhere between special and nothing special. At least the ones I've talked to. My gods are people, people I can relate to and sympathize with. Do you ever have any sympathy for your God?"

"You are confused, if I may say so, respectfully," said the shorter one.

The taller one produced a slim black rectangular object, about the size of a pack of cigarettes, and held it out before his chest.

"You have probably never seen one of these," the shorter one said. "With this, you can talk to God."

"Is that so?"

"We would like to leave this here with you overnight. Would that interest you? We could return at this time tomorrow to get it back and hear about your experience."

"How does it work?"

"You will find it is quite simple. After all, God is always listening. This just might help you believe that He hears you. I think you will discover it is rather different than talking to any of your gods here in town. We would like you to have a chance to connect with the giver of eternal life."

"You use this thing yourselves?"

"It is technically only for those who need the proof."

"Sure then, leave the box. I'll give it a whirl. You

boys come back by in the morning."

They stood up and I went and opened the front door. The taller one grinned again and his gold tooth flashed bright in the sunlight as he walked out. The shorter one stopped and put out his hand. As I shook it he said, "We do wish you luck and hope that you can make a connection." He then also left. I closed the door and ran to the bedroom and pulled back the curtain. I expected to see them get into a car or cross the street toward the next house. Did they have more God Boxes? I went back to the living room and saw the box resting on my coffee table.

My plan was to ignore the box until night but I couldn't resist. I picked up the little thing and felt that it was warm. I hesitated, then talked into it like a CB. "Hello?" I said.

"Ron," a voice said.

"My name is Rob."

"Rob," the voice said.

"You can hear me?"

"Yes, I hear you."

"You're a woman."

"I am everything."

"You speak English so well."

"Why should I not? I invented it."

"I guess I just thought you'd speak Arabic or Latin or Italian."

"I am of every race."

"What do you look like?"

"I appear as you imagine me. You do see me, do you not?"

"I think so. It's hard to imagine you look like I imagine you do."

"How do you imagine me?"

"Right now?"

"What is it that you need?"

"I don't know."

"You began to write something down this morning before you were interrupted."

"That's right."

"What was it?"

"Don't you know?"

"Whether I know or not is not important. It is important that you know what you wanted to say, and more importantly that you say it."

"You mean to you?"

"Writing it down is the same as telling me. Would you like to go back to your writing?"

"I'm enjoying talking to you."

"I know."

"Right."

"What would you like to talk about?"

"I sort of feel like I'm on the spot, y'know? Like this is confession or something."

"I do not want you to feel that way. I am just glad you are talking to me."

"I'm glad you're listening."

"I am always listening."

"I've heard. Do you know everything about me?"

"Of course, my son."

"Could you not call me that?"

"Of course."

"What color underwear am I wearing?"

"That is not *knowing* about you."

"Sure it is. That might say a lot about me. What kind of underwear are *you* wearing?"

"I do not think it is appropriate."

"Underwear or the question?"

"Hot pink panties, is that what you want to hear?"

"You said you were as I imagine you."

"As long as you believe, I suppose."

"I'm beginning to, but I have so many questions."

"One step at a time, my son. Sorry."

"Listen, where is this going?"

"Where do you want it to go?"

"Is this really all just up to me? Jesus! Sorry."

"That is OK. I understand your frustration."

"But there is so much frustration in the world—to mention one problem alone—can you understand it all?"

"I said one step at a time."

"Am I just a step?"

"Only if that is how you feel."

"God, that's so frustrating!"

"Is it? Sorry."

"What do you want from me?"

"For you to believe. I thought you knew that."

"But is that really enough? Maybe I want *you* to believe in *me*."

"Is there not something you want to tell me?"

"How do I hang up with you? How do I make this stop?"

"You only need to stop listening."

"You mean stop believing?"

"No, just stop listening."

"What if I just stop talking?"

"I will still be here."

"Can't I shut this thing off?"

"I told you how, but do you not want to talk?"

"I'm imagining you in that underwear. You have brown hair?"

"Yes."

"Is that your choice? Your preference?"

"Yes."

"Mine too."

"Yes."

"I'll bet you really know how to make people feel good."

"That is what I do best."

"I wish you could make me feel good."

"Do I not?"

"I wish you could make me feel *better*."

"I am sure I could, if you would let me."

"I'm here all by myself."

"I know."

"I've had a lot on my mind lately."

"Tell me about it."

"God, why do I keep having the same dreams all the time? With the shit everywhere and the airplane crashes. Are you putting that in my head?"

"No, that is all your doing."

"That's crazy, I hate those dreams!"

"You hate a lot. Hate has a way of staying with you, mostly when you do not want it."

"Where does it come from?"

"Arizona."

"What?"

"Nothing. You were simply talking about your dreams."

"Did you make France?"

"Is it not beautiful?"

"Did you make it?"

"Have you been?"

"No."

"It is beautiful."

I decided to stop listening to the box. My plan was to ignore it for good but I knew I didn't have a prayer. I went into the kitchen and piled ham on top of cheese on top of bread. I turned the radio on. I flipped for some jazz but found Linda Ronstadt singing about silver threads and golden needles. I remembered asking my mother once if she thought Linda Ronstadt was single. Linda Ronstadt is *my* age! she said. I didn't know what that had to do with being single or not, but I remember being shocked by the thought of Linda Ronstadt aging. Then for some reason that thought led to the thought of The Green Tavern in Gloucester, Massachusetts with its tiny glasses of beer. Then to my shitty posture. Then to Victor Hugo and the Hunchback of Notre Dame. And then to those clean young men. They would be back for her in the morning. They would want to know what happened. I wished I had some cocktail sauce. What's in that? What's that made of? I could make my own. Ketchup and horseradish? Lemon juice? Oh, fuck it. I turned the radio off. I ate my sandwich and tried to enjoy the silence.

BORN TOGETHER

I woke up early to sunlight and the Canadian national anthem playing in my head. I watch a lot of hockey so I often hear that song on TV. We live in (very) upstate New York, about ten minutes from the border of Ontario. My girlfriend yelled to me from the kitchen: Dom DeLuise has a Volkswagen! Although I might have misunderstood her. I rolled over and tried to go back to sleep, my right hand still fat and aching.

My girlfriend is incredible. She is pregnant and making breakfast. Her name is Uhln and she's beautiful. She has paper-white skin and wavy, long black hair. She's soft and small and elegant. She's read Moby-Dick twice. I love her so much. I've known Uhln since high school. In fact we dropped out of high school together. I consider us lucky to know what we want from life at this age, which most people consider young, but I'm sharp beyond my years. I know guys ten years older than me that are as dumb as toddlers. People can be pretty judgmental about our situation and our age and all, but things don't happen like they used to. We didn't plan on having a baby. Some things you expect and some things you don't, but life doesn't have to be all bad.

My name is Madrid. When they were twenty-five or so, my mom and dad got a chance to go to Europe with a jazz group. She was a singer and he played the drums. It was a low-budget thing but they got to see like four or five different countries. I was conceived in Spain, in Madrid. There is a town near here called Madrid but for some reason everyone pronounces it MAD-rid. Everyone in school, even the teachers, called me MAD-rid. So dumb. You should see this town we live in. I know people—I work with some of them—that graduated ten years ago and they're still the same dumb people they were in their senior year. Also, it's cold as shit here.

I couldn't go back to sleep but didn't really care. It's Sunday and I don't have to go to work. That's extra nice because it's February and twenty-below outside. Uhln said we were having a Swedish breakfast today as she brought over some crackers and cheese and cold cuts to the coffee table.

She may do some stuff around the house, but Uhln is eight months pregnant and I try to see that she doesn't have to do too much. She doesn't have a job and I try my best to take care of her. I work at the Ponderosa Steakhouse out on Route 37. Mostly I bus tables and do dishes, but sometimes they let me help with food prep if it's super busy. I've become pretty good friends with a guy that works in the kitchen there. His name is Tino. He's from Ghana or Guyana, I can never remember. His father is a doctor and he moved them here so he could open his own office. This town is cheap to live in and apparently competition between doctors isn't much. Besides, Tino told me his dad was a different kind of doctor than any other one here. One time I said: If your dad's a doctor he must be rich, so why are you working here? Tino told me his dad was definitely not rich but that even if he was he'd still make sure his son had a job. I asked Tino if his mom worked and he said he never knew his mom. He's three years older than me but I always felt like I was the older one. Tino has skin the color of butterscotch chips and he's about a foot taller than me. For some reason he doesn't have a girlfriend. Maybe it's the way he talks. Maybe girls can't understand him. I felt sad for Tino when I thought about what it would be like to have no mom. My parents live here in town and have all their lives. They're still together and are still in love. They met in junior high and got married after high school. I think that's why they understand how things are with Uhln and me. We're in love and they can see it because they know it. They help us with this apartment but they wish we'd get married.

I didn't have a bad childhood even though my parents were poor. I get the feeling they had potato chips for dinner sometimes so I could have new shoes. Sometimes I think that Uhln and I have it better off than my parents did when they were getting going. My dad had a shot later at a big break playing the jazz drums for a famous trumpet player but it never happened. Mom now works full-time as a shift manager at Ames. Dad's pretty sick now (cigarettes) and the bills have ruined any chance of their getting out of debt. I asked Tino once about his dad helping out my dad, since he's a doctor and all, and he told me that his dad is a doctor for crazy people. He moved to the right place, if you ask me.

Uhln's parents are still together, too. They have a lot of money but are not happy. It's obvious her mom married her dad for the money. They live in Boston and they're total assholes. They sent Uhln up to this crappy town when she was twelve. She'd been a troublemaker at a fancy private school so her folks made her come live here with her aunt, her mom's sister. They figured small town life would settle her down. They didn't know that you get into more trouble when you're bored and there's nothing to do. Anyway, her aunt's a bitch and we don't ever talk to her and Uhln got pregnant so I guess we showed her family a thing or two.

PEDDERSON'S UNCLE

Pedderson's uncle was an odd man but we liked going over to his house. His name was Myron Osgood and he was most often sitting at his desk, dunking chocolate bars into a mug of tequila and reading a newspaper, sometimes talking to it. Pedderson's mother didn't care much for her only sibling, or for us going to his house. She was never too hard on us though and I think she secretly liked the quiet time with us not around. Pedderson's dad had died in Korea. Myron Osgood had also been in Korea. We figured that Pedderson's mom would rather it have been her husband that came back alive.

I wasn't technically a family member, but Pedderson and I'd been best friends since the age of five. My mother had no boyfriend and no job and she got all her money from the drunk driver that jumped the curb and ran over and killed my dad as he was mowing the next door neighbor's lawn.

The next door neighbors had been in Hawaii and my mom said it should've been Mr. Houseman that was hit by the car. The Houseman's were lying on a beach in Oahu when my dad was squished to ground meat between an Oldsmobile and a Sears push-mower. My mom was never the same after that. She seemed to have no interest in anything except white wine, saltine crackers, and the television set.

Pedderson and I were the same age and both without fathers. That's another reason we liked to go to his uncle's house. We could ask him about girls and other stuff that boys are clueless about and he'd tell it to us straight. He probably said a lot of things that weren't true, but we liked it all the same. Penny, Pedderson's mother, was nothing like my mother. She was fun and still had her looks and she laughed and made jokes. She was very nice to us and would fix snacks whenever we wanted. We used to play a good deal of pranks on Penny and if she ever did realize we were the culprits the punishment was always light. For instance, Pedderson would have to do the dishes and I would dry them and put them away, or he'd wash the clothes and I'd hang them up to dry. I always got the drying part because I wasn't a blood relative. Even if I'd not been included in the sentencing I would've helped my friend serve his time.

One time I pulled a one-man job on Penny without

Pedderson knowing. Late one afternoon we'd been at Uncle Myron's house where he had let us both dip chocolate bars into his tequila. When we got home Penny smelled the booze on us and said we were forbidden to ever go back to Myron's house. Pedderson didn't seem too upset. I guess he thought she'd get over it in a few days and he could soon go back to his uncle's, but I took it personally. She wasn't my real mom and had no right to tell me what to do. Penny was upstairs and Pedderson had gone to take a piss when I took his mother's car keys and dumped them into my backpack. We watched TV for a while and then Penny made us nachos. We told her we were sorry for what we'd done and she said that she forgave us and then gave us each a big hug. We had hugged and made up so I said goodbye and went home.

Pedderson and I always walked to school together. The next morning he was not on the corner waiting for me as he usually was. I waited for a few minutes and then thought I'd better get going or I was going to be late. When I got to our classroom Pedderson wasn't there and I stared at his empty desk wondering where he could be. I opened my backpack to get my notebook out and I saw Penny's car keys sitting at the bottom. I forgot that I'd put them there, that I had stolen them from her. She probably needs her car keys to drive to work, I thought. She is probably yelling at

Pedderson right now and making him turn the house upside-down to help her find the missing keys. Our teacher, Ms. Dent, never believed anything we students said but I considered telling her the truth to see if she'd let me leave. Instead, I told her that I felt like throwing up and I needed to go see the nurse. She wrinkled up her mouth more than I thought possible and said she didn't believe me. I squeezed my stomach and asked her if she'd rather me throw up on her classroom floor. She sent me to the nurse's office and didn't ask why I was taking my backpack with me. I left school and walked straight to Pedderson's house where of course Penny's car was in the driveway. The front door was unlocked and I figured her house keys were in my backpack, too. There was nobody there so I walked to Uncle Myron's place.

I had never seen his car move before, but Myron's car was not in the driveway when I got there. I knocked on the front door and Uncle Myron opened it, wearing a pink bathrobe and holding a mug in his hand. He said good morning son and I asked him if Pedderson was inside. He told me no and said wasn't this quite a day we were having so far. I asked him what he meant and he said that Pedderson and his mother had come over in a fuss, needing to borrow the car. Myron invited me inside and inside I went. He

89

offered me coffee and I said that I didn't drink coffee but what I did want was to know what had happened this morning. I sat on the couch and Myron came and sat next to me. He hitched up the hem of his robe to his knees and I saw that it wasn't coffee he had in his mug. He told me that Penny had rushed over to his house yelling that she needed his car so she could get Pedderson to school and herself to work. They were both running very late. I asked him if everything worked out OK. He said he gave them the car and off they went. That was all he knew. I told Uncle Myron I felt sick and that I had a confession to make. I unzipped my backpack and held up the keys. I told him that I had stolen Penny's keys yesterday as a joke but then forgot about it until this morning. He stared at me with wide eyes and frowned. Then he jumped up and let out a big rolling laugh. His hairy chest peeked through the long "v" in his robe and he lifted the mug to his chapped lips. His laughter echoed inside the mug and I could hear him drinking between breaths. I felt so guilty about the problems I'd caused that I began to cry. Myron stopped his laughing and sat down again beside me. He put his arm around me and told me to have a drink from his mug. I took it in my hands with a sob and he smiled at me and nudged the mug with his hand from its bottom up to my mouth. As the drink was pushed to my face I didn't like the smell but I closed my eyes and gulped down the entire thing. I felt even more guilt but Myron looked satisfied. He told me he wanted to show me something and pulled me up by my arm and escorted me into his den.

Uncle Myron set me in a big leather chair then disappeared briefly. He returned with two mugs, set them on a table next to the chair then went to a bookshelf. I had never been in this room before and as I looked around I saw lots of photos in frames and books everywhere and vases with fresh flowers in them all around. In a picture frame next to the mugs I saw two men. One of them was obviously a young Myron and he had his arm around the other man. They were both smiling and were both wearing military outfits.

"Is this you in Korea?"

"It certainly is."

He said the other man in the photo was Pedderson's dad.

"That photo was taken just a few days before he was killed. He was my best friend."

He said that they had been so close that Pedderson's mom hated him for it. He said that's what he wanted to show me as he sat down on the arm of the chair close to me and opened a battered photo album. He went through dozens of pictures of him and Pedderson's dad in Korea and told me that he'd never loved a man more.

"I've never known a man more brave and strong and handsome."

"What happened to him?"

"He was shot in the head."

He said that when Pedderson's dad was brought back to their camp in a helicopter, he didn't even recognize him when he saw him. He was dead when they brought him in on the stretcher.

"Seeing a man so beautiful blown open made me want to kill myself."

"My father was killed, too."

Not by a gun in Korea I told him, but by a man in a car on his way home from a tavern at three o'clock in the afternoon.

"I know, son. I bet you loved your dad."

THE HOLIDAY DANCE

"That's a really depressing story," she said without laughing.

"Come on, I thought you'd find that funny," Max said.

"You need a girlfriend."

"Oh, loosen up."

Max wished that she were his girlfriend and he wasn't sure why he'd told her that story. Sofia had always been a good friend. It wasn't her fault that he was in love with her any more than it was his fault she'd never love him.

"Oh, I'm about to be late," she said. "I need to go. Thanks for the coffee. See you later in the week?" Sofia stood up and grabbed her coat off the back of her chair. "Yeah, I'll see you later. But I got that thing Thursday though," Max said. "Oh, right," she said, turning her head to say good luck before walking out.

When Sofia had first walked in and sat down at the

table with Max she had a big smile on her face and he noticed how her green sweater matched her eyes. He almost resented their friendship. She told Max she was excited about a guy she'd met while visiting her parents in Pennsylvania. The son of her parents' friends. "You'd like him," Sofia said. "I'll bet," Max said. The guy was starting his own company.

When she asked if Max had done anything fun over the holidays, he told her that he'd spent most of the time with his mom and dad upstate. One night though he met up with some old high school friends. They'd gone out to a strip club, he told her—The Mouse's Ear. Max's parents, as they did every year, had given him lots of Hanukkah gelt, both in the form of a hefty roll of cash and also the usual chocolate coins. Max's pockets were stuffed when he and his friends went to the club. He'd decided after a few vodkas to get a lap dance. The girl was pretty and Max got excited. She pushed her breasts into his face and put all the weight of her back end onto Max's thighs. The dancer thrust her crotch into Max's belt buckle. It was hot and Max got sweaty. When the song came to an end the stripper gave Max a kiss on the cheek then stood up and waited. He reached into his right front pocket and felt it was sticky. He pulled out his cash and it was covered in gooey melted chocolate coins. The girl didn't seem fazed. Max made a point to tell her it was chocolate. She said to follow her and they went to the bar where together they wiped off each bill with a clean damp bar rag. The girl even had the bartender buy Max a beer. When two hundred dollars in twenties were all good as new the girl said with a smile, "Money's money, honey," and jiggled off for the next dance.

Sofia looked at Max a bit crooked then opened her mouth to speak.

DON'T FORGET THE DILL

One of the jobs I hated most at that place was peeling the hard-boiled eggs. We used them for egg salad sandwiches. I'd have to do like thirty or forty at a time and I'd just rip those things to bits. The manager said to peel them under running water and that would help. I don't think it did. Sometimes though I'd get one that would peel like a dream. The shell would slide right off in what felt like one whole piece, like slipping a sock off your foot. It was magical. That was rare though and it was mostly me tapping each egg all over with my knuckle, breaking the shell in a thousand tiny cracks, then growing more and more frustrated with each one. I'd eventually just be grabbing at fragments of shell, dragging along chunks of tender profitable egg white, throwing it all down into the sink. The egg salad was pretty good though. Celery, grated red onion (so you get the juice), a little Dijon mustard, paprika, dill, salt, loads of cracked black pepper, and a bucket of mayo.

I'd finished my first year of college and felt a little dumb working there with the high school girls. But they were nice and apart from the eggs I wasn't terrible at my job. It was a family run place and the daughter, my manager, was good to me. Their name was Benedict. She was Jenny Benedict. She was my age and also in college. She had lovely long smooth brown legs. I called her Legs Benedict. She never seemed to mind but I found it extra funny when the egg-peeling task was first assigned to me. Looking back, I think we really liked each other. One time she and one of the other girls were going to see a movie after work and they invited me to come. When I went out to the parking lot Jenny was by herself smoking a cigarette in her car. She asked if I was ready and I asked where Morgan was. She said Morgan had to leave and it would just be us. During the movie—I'm sure it was with James Woods and Michael J. Fox—we held hands, rubbed inseams, and kissed. I think her tongue was in my ear before the previews ended. From then on we'd make out in the walk-in fridge at work and find a way to touch one another whenever we passed by. We never went out outside of the sandwich shop on a date again. We just kind of became horny co-workers. I was fine with that. Maybe it's because we knew we'd be separated in the fall. Maybe we just didn't know what to do with it all. I never gave it much thought until I started going with my first real girlfriend sophomore year. I compared her to Jenny in my mind all the time.

Things kept on that way for nearly the rest of the summer until mid-August when Jenny burned her hand pretty bad at the deep fryer and stopped coming to work for a while. It wasn't but a few days before I was meeting Morgan in the walk-in fridge. The day Jenny came back to work she found first thing me and Morgan in the fridge with our shorts unzipped and kissing. Legs Benedict fired me on the spot.

Anyway, that's what I think about sometimes when I boil an egg now.

BULLSEYE

Everyone saw Sawyer as a tough guy. His head was shaved bald and he put his lit cigarette behind his ear when he threw darts. He spent a lot of time at the bar for someone who didn't drink. Maybe he'd quit booze some time ago. Maybe he just loved darts—he was the best in our league. Rumors said that he'd once set fire to the 9th Precinct and that he'd once killed a neighbor's dog. Another one was that a kid tried to mug him, but with his keys sticking out between his fingers Sawyer punched the kid's eye out. The story went that as the kid was holding his face, bleeding on the sidewalk, Sawyer said, "When you grow up people will ask what happened to your eye. You can tell them that when you were younger you were a real piece of shit." These rumors didn't seem to fit the soft-spoken Sawyer but maybe that's what made them kind of believable.

Sawyer's wife spent a lot of time at the bar. There

weren't many rumors about her because her life was pretty much right there for everyone to see. Analee drank too much. Every night that she and Sawyer were out together she'd get drunk and take her top off or rub people's crotches under the bar or try and get an argument going with somebody. It wasn't uncommon for her to come over during a darts tournament and yell something at Sawyer like, "There's a guy here that wants to screw me! What're you gonna do about it!" Sawyer would just put his burning cigarette behind his ear and throw a perfect round. By night's end he'd scoop up Analee and carry her home. No one knew how long they had been married. They both looked to be in their mid-forties. They both had many tattoos and many were the same. They didn't have any kids but they had a fat tabby cat that spent so much time on their front stoop they finally named it Furburger.

We won the Division C championships that year I was on the team. Furburger is surely dead now. Who knows about Sawyer and Analee. I may have been the worst darts player but I still have the trophy with all our names on it. And I've quit smoking since then.

DC-3

The Carlton Arms Hotel is under construction for some extensive renovations so I've been able to get an affordable room. It's nearly midnight and thankfully, even during the repairs, the hotel bar is still open. The barkeep is a friendly fellow who's been working here for half a century. He handsomely wears a white collared shirt, red vest, and black bowtie. By my guess he's 70 years old. He's quizzing me on historical facts and telling me ghost stories about the hotel's long past days of fame. It's only the two of us in here and I sit quietly across from him, looking down at my book, reading the same sentence over and over as he continuously feeds a tour guide monologue into the top of my head. He carries on about politicians and peculiar guests who have stayed upstairs, famous people who sat right where I'm sitting, and all the unknown city secrets that hold infinitely more fascinating details than the grade school legacy everyone comes here to meditate upon. I've not gotten up and walked out yet because every time I empty my glass he automatically refills it without pausing between words. By my guess I'm on my fifth. It briefly annoys me that I've apparently come all this way just to sit at a bar. But I know there is more than enough time. Besides, I needed a break from my wife and New York, and I haven't been to Washington, DC since I was a kid.

"This next drink is on the house," he offers, "if you can tell me who that lady in the painting on the back wall is." I turn around to see the one of four portraits in the room he is referring to.

"Dolley Madison," I say. He fills my glass again.

"Which room are you in?"

"8," I said.

"That's good."

He proceeded to let me know that the former head-vice-secretary of something or other jumped out of the bedroom window in room 19 and died with a messy splat like a rotten cantaloupe onto K Street. I continued reading as I finished the drink. After a slow paragraph my eyes got dry and the blurred words began to scatter and quickly crawl off the page like cockroaches. I fell off my stool. The gentleman helped me to my feet and said, "I think you'd better get to your room. I have to close up here anyway."

"Ok, but give me the rest of that bottle to take with me."

He looked around. We were definitely alone.

"I'll give it to you, but only if you promise to go straight up to bed."

I promised.

I woke the next day with the previous night's train ride running through my aching head. The trip was uneventful apart from an acquaintance I made passing through Delaware. I assumed she'd just boarded in Wilmington as she approached me with exasperation, dragging a large suitcase. There were plenty of vacant seats and I was solely occupying what was situated like a restaurant booth that could accommodate a party of four. I was hunched over a newspaper at the white tabletop when she dropped her luggage down and collapsed next to it. She was directly across from me. "It feels good to sit down," she said. About three minutes later she spoke again. Her name, she told me, was "Anna Whitman, Whitman like the chocolates."

I hesitated and then suggested, "Or like Walt."

"Or like that guy who shot all those people at that school in Texas," she said.

I pursed my lips and went back to the paper, but something about her kept me distracted. With my head still bowed I raised my eyes to see her face. As she stared out the window I studied her profile and discovered a bizarre familiarity. She had a remarkable resemblance to me—the same pale complexion and an identical turned-up nose. We both had dark squinty eyes and short brown hair. She was wearing no make-up and I felt uncomfortably odd admiring her, wondering what she looked like underneath her clothes. I'd been examining her for a while when she turned to me and asked, out of a mouth like my own, "Have you been on this train since New York?" I said, "Yes," and she said, "me too." I was a bit confused and told her I thought she'd gotten on at the last stop. "Uh-uh," she said, "I just haven't been able to find anywhere I wanted to sit. I guess it's impossible to stay still on a moving train, eh?" Anna lit a cigarette and asked if I lived in DC. I replied with a polite, "No." She took a long drag and said, "Well then, how about your name?" I lied and told her my name was James Madison. She smiled real wide and said, "Like the President!" I said, "Yes, I suppose so," and then told her I was going to sleep. As my eyes closed I saw Anna Whitman curiously looking me over.

I was awakened by her tapping me on the arm, whispering that we'd arrived. Anna followed me off of the train and into the station. "Well, Mr. President," she announced, "here we are." She handed me a folded piece of paper, winked at me, and then walked away. I opened the note to find that it was, apart from a phone number written in ink, blank stationery from the Carlton Arms Hotel. By the time I looked up, she'd disappeared with her big suitcase. I hadn't yet made arrangements for where I'd be staying so I got a taxi to the Carlton Arms, checked into the smallest room, paid for the whole week in advance, and got drunk.

As I lay aching in the bed in room 8 I felt an urge to be upright. I could tell that I'd slept through the whole morning. I went downstairs, back into the bar. There was my friend from last night. "I hope you got some rest," he said with judgmental concern. "Are you going to be staying here long?"

"That depends," I said.

"On what?"

"On the service."

Pouring me a hot coffee he said, "My name is Rudy, and when Rudy is on duty you're all set."

"That's good news, Rudy."

After a sip I asked him what time it was. "Just past two," he told me. I looked deep into the steaming black coffee. I could feel the heat opening the pores in my face.

My headache was nearly defeated.

"Hey Rudy, is there a girl staying here?" I'd wanted to ask him last night but was hesitant to create the conversation.

"There's not many guests here right now," he said, "I think the only girl is the little Stadler child."

"No, I mean, is there a girl staying here alone, about my age?"

"Let's see," he said. "There was a young woman here for a while. Last month. I believe she was in your room. Number 8."

"Is that so?" I found that to be suspiciously coincidental. "What did she look like?"

"Well, she was tall. And skinny. Real white. Pretty face. Short hair, like a boy's."

"Do you know her name?"

"No, she never came in here. I don't get to know people's names unless they come in for a drink. What's your name anyhow?"

I stuck with James Madison. No comment from Rudy. I showed him the piece of paper that Anna had given me.

"Do you recognize that phone number? Is it the number of this hotel?"

"Nope and nope," he said.

Finishing my coffee I thought it was time I get outside.

It's early April in DC and there are murmurs of cherry blossoms in the street. The weather is still cool as spring has yet to drag in. The air burns my nose and causes my cheeks to tighten. This town is one giant cemetery; one giant landmark; one great big memorial. From outside the Carlton Arms I can survey the white peaks of the marble tombstones that rise up and tower over the less important dead of Washington. I pull my coat collar tight under my chin.

After an hour of walking and an hour in Henry Knox Books, I make my way to the Smithsonian Air and Space Museum and go straight to the airplanes; I always liked them best. I never was too interested in the outer space stuff because it seemed so distant, so not a part of my life that it could ever be real. My favorite airplane is the Eastern Airlines DC-3. It's enormous, with fat engines, and it's all bright shining silver. Rounding the corner I see it hanging in the sky. I've never been on an airplane. The idea of being thousands of feet off the ground and landing in a far off city in a matter of hours causes my mind to wander. Staring up at the belly of the plane I try to imagine what it must feel like to pilot something of this size. Taking off with great speed and watching everything you're leaving behind shrink and fade away. That's a feeling I'd like to know some day. I explore the rest of the museum, eat a hamburger, and decide to walk back to the hotel. It's getting dark.

Ascending the stairs inside the Carlton Arms I can see the door of my room slightly open with light peeking into the hallway. I remember closing it. When I reach the top of the steps I cautiously push the door and widen the crack enough to stick my head in. There I see Rudy leaned up comfortably on my bed, asleep, with a book in his lap.

"Rudy!" I obviously startled him and he jumped with a jolt of confusion. I notice on the table that the bottle of J&B from last night is empty. I don't remember finishing it.

"I'm sorry, Jim, I must've fallen asleep!"

"What are you doing in here?"

"I came up to return your book and then you weren't here and your door was open and I just started looking through the book and I guess I fell asleep."

"Did you drink the rest of that whiskey, too?"

Standing up he said, "No sir, I think you probably managed that on your own."

"What book are you talking about?"

"The one you were reading, downstairs last night,

you left it on the bar."

"Oh. Why didn't you give it to me this morning?"

"I forgot. But I also came up to tell you that that girl came this afternoon, the one that was staying here."

"The girl I asked you about?"

"I guess so. She came into the bar and asked if somebody was here that looked like you. She knew your name, too."

"What did you tell her?"

"I told her there was a young man here that fit the description. She said she'd come back later."

"When later? Tonight?"

"I don't know. It's not really my business now is it?"

"Aren't you supposed to be working?"

"Aw, there ain't nobody down there."

I opened the door and made a waving gesture with my hand. He walked out, stopped and said, "You'll come down for a drink later?"

"Yeah, I'll be down," I said, and shut the door.

I stretched out on the bed and rested for a while. The phone number from Anna was on the nightstand. I opened the paper and studied it, feeling excited that she'd come looking for me. There was a telephone at the end of the hall and I decided to utilize it. I dropped a coin in and dialed.

After five rings a man's voice answered. I could hear a noisy gathering in the background, like a party.

"Hello? Yes?"

"I'm calling for Anna."

"Who's calling?"

"I am. Is she there?"

"Anna's not here."

I heard forks striking plates and glasses clinking together. He was talking loudly but I figured it wasn't directed at me, he was just trying to speak over the commotion.

"Do you know when I can reach her?"

"No, I don't."

"Is this where she lives?"

"What is it that you want?"

"I want to speak with Anna."

"She's not here."

"I understand that."

He didn't say anything.

"Just tell her the President called," I said, and hung up.

I got my book from my room and went back down to the bar where Rudy seemed to have returned to some semblance of professionalism.

"How are you, Mr. Madison?"

"I'm fine, Rudy."

Setting a drink in front of me he said, "Do you know what they found in Lincoln's pockets when he was shot?"

"Yes, I do."

"Confederate money! Can you believe that?" he said with a crazy laugh, slapping the bar.

"Listen Rudy, what else did that girl say that came in this afternoon? Did she tell you her name?"

"No. She wasn't here but a minute and she didn't have much to say except asking about you."

"Strange," I said.

"What's that book you've been reading? I saw my name in it. Is it about somebody named Rudy?"

"Actually, there is someone named Rudy in it."

"Ha! I'm famous. What's he like?"

"He's not such a nice guy. He steals all his brother's money and then kills him and runs off with the widow. It's not very original."

Rudy looked disappointed as he told me he had to go to the basement to get more champagne. "Who's drinking champagne?" I asked. "You never know who might come in," he said as he left, "You got to always be ready." The amber whiskey in my glass, backlit by a candle, was melted gold and it sparkled in my eyes and made me warm and lonely at the same time. I leaned onto the bar and opened my book.

A moment later someone sat on the stool next to me. Of course it was her. "I called you tonight," I said, swiveling to face her. She looked just like she did on the train. Not that I expected her to look differently, but I guess I didn't know what to expect at all. She smiled with half her mouth and said, "Anything for the First Lady?" I got up and went behind the bar and poured Anna a drink. I asked her who the man was that answered the phone when I called. "How should I know?" she said, raising her glass to me.

"Is that where you live, where I called?"

"Sort of."

"Why were you staying here at the hotel last month?"

"Well I had to stay *somewhere*. Are these really the things you want to know about me? Where do *you* live? Why are *you* staying here?"

I told her that I live in New York and that I came to DC to kill some time. I said I was at the Carlton Arms because of her. "That's funny," she said, "I was on my way back from New York when I met you. I hadn't been there since I was a kid." She took a drink and as I was considering asking her for more information she started talking again.

The phone number she gave me was indeed where she lived, at her house that she shared with her husband. She told me she was leaving him. I thought perhaps she'd wanted me to call her house just to make her husband jealous. As she stared into her glass I stared at her. It was uncanny how much we looked alike. I wondered if she'd noticed it too. How could she not? Either way, I'd decided to stay at the Carlton Arms for as long as my money would hold out.

"Will you go with me to the museum tomorrow?"

"Which one?"

"The one with the airplanes."

She nodded yes and then leaned over and kissed me on the mouth.

"Where are you staying tonight? Do you have to go home?"

"No. There's a party at my house and I hate everyone there. They'll be at it until sunrise."

"Perfect."

We stood up at the same time. I followed Anna as she led the way up to room 8. When I let her into our room I realized that I'd left my book downstairs again. I went back down to the bar and picked up my book. On the way out I saw the portrait of Dolley Madison glaring at me. I walked over and got up real close to the painting. "Dolley, honey,"

I said. "We're going to be awake all night. Tell Rudy to make sure he has the coffee ready first thing in the morning."

When I got back up to the room, Anna was standing naked in front of the mirror. I removed all of my clothes and wrapped my arms around her from behind. Our bodies were exact. Our reflection showed just one person. Anna. I knew what she was seeing, and that's when she noticed.

"We are identical."

Anna put her arms behind her so that her hands met at the bottom of my spine. I tightened my grip around her and felt her pull me in with surprising strength. Our skin was hot. I could not tell her body from mine. As she held me harder I forced myself into her more. My muscles began to tremble and I felt faint. But quickly everything became clear. I could now see us, only me, in the mirror.

ARIGATO, HERNANDO-SAN

It was the first time I'd used a temp agency, and so far the last. Hernando and I got the job on the same day through the same agency. We were hired as sales clerks. It was a fancy shop on Madison Avenue that sold expensive teapots and teacups and flower vases and such, all from Japan. I remember a cast iron incense burner that was selling for $250. I never sold it. Hernando and I were the only males at the store, and we became friendly, though not exclusively for this reason. Business seemed slow but the store brought on extra help each year for the holidays as policy. We had to wear all black to work. No jeans. I tried black jeans once a week but was told each time not to wear them again. Four out of five days I wore the same black slacks, and every day I wore a black collared shirt that was too big for me. It looked like a garbage bag. Hernando wore mostly the same clothes every day too. I figured, like me, he didn't have a lot of options and just washed his clothes on his days off. Since the shop was usually quiet, Hernando and I spent much of the day standing at the big front window watching the people move up and down Madison Avenue. We'd elbow each other at pretty girls and sneer at the rich.

There was one reasonable bar in the neighborhood and I'd pop in after work a few days each week. The bartender was the same every time I went in. He was French. His name was Guy. He said it was pronounced "Ghee" but I called him "Guy" like it's said in English. I think Guy also enjoyed watching the Madison Avenue people. I asked Hernando once or twice a week to come have a beer with me after work but he never did.

One afternoon I was standing with Hernando at the store window when he looked at his watch to see if we were close to lunch break. It looked like a new watch. "Is that a new watch?" I said. I didn't know much about watches but I knew that Cartier meant expensive. That store was right across the street. "I've had it a while," he said. A week later Hernando pulled out his wallet to show me a picture of his niece. It was a shiny leather Gucci wallet with the distinct red and green stripes I saw in the Gucci store window every day on my way to work. I'd never seen him with that wallet before. Soon after that Hernando came to work in new black clothes. I knew he was making the same money as me at the shop. Maybe he had other money. I asked Hernando if he wanted to join me for a beer after work. He surprised me that day by saying yes.

We sat down at the bar and I introduced Hernando and Guy. We got two beers and Guy disappeared. Hernando glanced at his Cartier watch. "Got somewhere to be?" I asked. "I can have one or two," he said. It wasn't my business but we were getting to know each other so I asked where it was he had to go. I knew he lived alone. I knew he didn't have a girlfriend. "I have to see someone later," he said. Maybe he was a drug dealer. "Do you have a date or something?" I said. "I just have to see someone," he said. He wasn't annoyed but I let it go. We sat in silence for a few sips. "I like this place," Hernando said. "Yeah, me too," I said. "Guy seems cool," he said. "Yeah, he is," I said. We talked about the Mets for a while and Guy brought over two more beers.

The next morning Hernando didn't show up for work. The store manager said she hadn't heard from him but that she planned to call his apartment if he wasn't in by 9:30. At 9:45 I asked if there was any news and she told me no. I stood at the front window by myself for most of the day. Usually we had our lunch delivered but I felt like getting outside. I had a half-hour break either way. It was sunny and I decided to walk over to Neil's Coffee Shop. I ordered a tuna melt with vegetable soup and coffee. As I ate I thought about my brother who was getting a divorce. I thought about myself and how long I would be working at the Japanese shop. I looked around at the other tables and saw that it was only people eating alone. Each one of them staring down at their food. I paid at the front and started walking back. As I passed the Chanel store I happened to look in through the window. I saw Hernando in there. He was with a woman who was holding a dress up to her body. It was Mrs. Arbiter. One of our most obnoxious customers. We made fun of her all the time. What was he doing with her and why wasn't he at work? I knocked on the window and he turned his head to see me. Mrs. Arbiter was blabbing her mouth and looking down at her shoes. Hernando's eyes widened then he sharply motioned with his thumb for me to scram. I got back to work ten minutes over my break. At the end of the day I went to Guy's expecting to see Hernando for an explanation. I ordered a second beer thinking he might come in at any moment. He knew where to find me. I gave up and left and walked toward the subway. It began to snow. The stores were lit up extra bright for Christmas and were filled with people. Not like our store.

The next morning Hernando again didn't show up for work. The manager again knew nothing. Around 11:30 he walked into the shop wearing blue jeans and a red sweater. The manager came over to tell him he was no longer needed. "I understand," he said, "but is it OK if I take him to lunch?" Hernando, who'd just gotten fired, asked if there was anywhere I felt like going. I said let's go to Guy's. Over two beers Hernando laid out the situation for me.

"Mrs. Arbiter!" I said, "Jesus, how old is she?"

"I don't know," he said. "50? 60? Who cares? I got a whole brand new hi-fi stereo at home. It's crazy. She begs for it. All I got to do is give it to her a few times a week."

"Is she married?"

"Probably. You wouldn't believe what she wants me to do."

The next week Mrs. Kreider came in and bought a large porcelain vase. She always touched my arm whenever she asked me the price of something. She sometimes called me honey. I knew she only lived a few blocks away and I asked her if instead of taking it with her she'd like me to personally deliver the heavy vase to her apartment later that afternoon.

SEVERANCE

"My God, it's like a country song," Shepherd said to himself. Staring at the letter on his kitchen table he began to sing, "I got laid off and my girlfriend's gone, I'm all alone and the rain's comin' down." He laughed out loud and it felt good. He read over the words on the paper again. The "Separation Date" was April 9th and if he continued to "perform his duties in a satisfactory manner," Shepherd would be paid a lump sum severance of $1,000. April 9th was one month away. That was easy enough. As he slouched in the hard chair Shepherd thought about how he'd spent most of his life trying to make other people happy. Alone in the kitchen, trying to focus on the coming weeks, his mind drifted to when he was fourteen and his mother left his father. When his mother left, she left Shep with a father that had no idea of how to do anything but go to work. A lot of people were getting laid off. Not enough money to pay the workers or whatever else the bosses could think of. He liked where he worked. Well, as much as anyone can like going to work but that's the way life is. You try and find something you can stand just enough to keep doing without going crazy.

He saw no reason that he wouldn't get the $1,000 so he considered himself to be in possession of a lot of money. He planned to make the money last. It seemed that many things in Shep's life went fast. His girlfriend left three weeks ago. He'd tried to make her happy but hadn't noticed that she was someone who could never be happy. He thought about calling her and telling her he'd come into some money but he knew better. Shep clicked on the radio. The setting sun was cutting through the rain and the fading light from the window seemed to swell and dim with the violins. Shep leaned back and decided not to think about anything. Tomorrow after all was just another day at work.

One month later a few guys from the plant took Shep out for some burgers after his last shift. He'd heard that a lot of people were losing their jobs but it seemed like he was the only one he knew of. Shep's old friend Troy was there. Troy had grown up with him and they'd gotten into a fair amount of mischief as boys but ended up nothing more than co-workers as they got older and got sucked into their separate lives. Shep couldn't help but wonder why Troy got to keep his job. He didn't see any difference in the work they both did. He felt like Troy had somehow cheated him. He could have raised a fuss at the foreman but what good would that do? He would've just made himself look foolish. He had the $1,000 check in his pocket and he tried to think about better things.

Early the next morning, Saturday, April 10, Shep woke up, went into his bathroom and splashed some cold water on his face over the sink. The pink wallpaper and the pink porcelain fixtures looked gray. On the bathroom window sill Shep saw a crusty dead bumblebee the size of his thumb, wings up, ready for take-off. The big bee was rolling back and forth against the screen from the breeze blowing in and out. He remembered his mother taking him as a child to see a magician in town that could bring back flies from the dead. The magician had a paper cup full of dead flies and one by one he would revive them with a wave of his hand and they'd fly out of the cup and off back into life.

It was a clear day and felt like it might be a hot one later. Before going to the bank, Shep stopped into Martin's Diner for coffee. Lucy, Martin's mother, was behind the counter and tended to Shep like he was family. Lucy had heard about his job and gave him a piece of pie on the house.

He wanted to bury his face into her greasy apron and cry himself back to sleep. The pie was better than he thought it'd be and he ate it too fast. Lucy got a napkin and wiped the blueberry from his chin. He thanked her, paid for his coffee leaving a tip, and walked to the Wells Fargo bank down the street.

The bank was empty and Shep went straight up to the teller. "Well hi, Shepherd. What can we do for you?" The bank teller was Tommy Grables. This was a small town and everyone grew up together. Shep said, "I got this check here from work, Tommy." "Alright, fine," said Tommy, who'd no doubt heard about Shep's job, too. "Do you want to open an account?" "No," Shep said, "better just give it to me in cash." "Ok, but don't you go spending this all in one place," said Tommy with a laugh. Shep didn't smile and Tommy quickly stopped his chuckling. Counting out the bills Tommy concentrated looking down. Shep stared at him and remembered that they were never friends in school. Tommy had once pushed Shep to the ground at a football game in front of a girl. This was the Tommy that Shep thought of right now. As Tommy slid the cash forward Shep wanted to pull him over the counter and shove the money into his mouth. "Here you go, a thousand bucks on the nose," Tommy said. "Thanks," Shep said, and turned and walked out the bank door.

It's a special feeling to have a pocket full of money and nowhere to go. Shep tried to enjoy having no real responsibilities but he was nervous about his new future. His father was dead and he had no clue where his mother was so he was spared feeling guilty for not giving his parents any money. He didn't have any brothers or sisters. If he did, he figured they'd probably have more money than he did anyway. Maybe he should go find an old motorcycle to buy and just ride straight on for as long as he wanted until he felt like stopping.

After walking a few blocks he came across a shop he'd never noticed before. A sign in the window announced: "The Finest Imported Articles From Europe." Shep went inside. He walked around the store, looking at all the attractive items for sale. There were silk scarves, gold-plated brooches, jewelry boxes, leather shoes, belts, and fancy shirts and dresses. He'd passed by a green velvet suit three times before he surprised himself by asking to try it on. The soft, dark material seemed to glow and it was comforting just to look at.

The suit fit. Shep felt his muscles relax and his skin get warm. He asked the old man behind the counter what it cost. "Nine hundred," the man said. "Nine hundred dollars?"

Shep said. "Try the hat," the man said, handing Shep a matching fedora. "Came in yesterday," the man said, "from Italy." Shep looked at himself in a mirror. "You can have it all for a grand," the man said. "Okay," Shep said. He gave the man his thousand dollars and said he'd wear the suit out. Shep told the man he could have his old clothes and said, "Maybe these are worth something."

Shep took a bus out to Troy's house. There were five other people on the bus and he felt them admiring him in his suit, maybe thinking he was on his way out of town for some big business. When he got to the house he leaned against a truck parked on the street and smoked a cigarette. It didn't look like Troy was home but he'd already made up his mind not to step onto the porch and knock on the door. He decided he had nothing to say to Troy. Shep walked all the way back into town. He approached Martin's Diner but didn't want to go inside. He wasn't hungry and he knew that Lucy wouldn't approve of his buying the suit. He thought about calling his girlfriend.

Shep just went on home. He went into his bathroom and used the pink toilet. He saw the lifeless bumblebee in the window. He gently picked it up by the wing, put it in his palm and carried it into the kitchen. Setting the bee on the table he took a glass from the cupboard and filled it full of cold milk. He dropped the dead insect into the glass. The milk seemed to bubble slightly around the fat bee. Shep took a sip. The milk was getting warm and it sent a signal of aliveness into his bones. He took a big gulp, the bee now floating in an inch of milk. The last gulp sent the bee swimming into Shep's mouth. He swirled the giant bug around. He began to feel his whole body buzzing—his brain, his veins. He opened his mouth and the bumblebee shot out and then hovered in front of his face. Shep lifted up and tipped his new green velvet fedora to the bee as it flew off into the other room and out through the still open front door.

I GUESS HE'S JUST RALPH THEN

There was an older man that was always at that bar on Sunset Boulevard every night we went in, which was nearly every night. We called him Mr. Furley because he looked like the landlord character Don Knotts played on Three's Company. You know. He was clearly there trying to get boys in their twenties to go back to his apartment. Oh, the silk scarves and floral prints and polyester. Truly. He was always a bit weird and forward but he was nice about it. It was obvious he was lonely.

Then there was that one night we went in and Mr. Furley wasn't there. He was always there. It didn't seem right without him there, which if nothing else is a testament to his reputation. I asked the bartender where the man was and he said, "Didn't you see the news? He's dead." I said that I had not seen the news and I asked how he died and what was his real name. The bartender said, "That old fruit? Who cares!

He's lucky we even let him in here."

That took me from one level of sadness at learning he'd died, to a whole lower hell of sorrow that someone would think and talk that way of him, and even think that way at all about any human.

At that moment I wished one night I'd gone home drunk with Mr. Furley and given him a hand job, then made him breakfast in the morning. That's not pity and I'm no hero, especially since I never did it. But we all deserve love or companionship, if only in a flash. I know I do.

A SHORT TRIP

Jerry and Gary weren't friends just because their names rhymed. They'd gone to junior high and high school together, played in a crappy band together. Both were on the baseball team. They'd both dated Patricia. Gary took her virginity but it was Jerry that married her. Gary had later also gotten married. The two men still lived in the same town but had such separate lives now that they could've lived a thousand miles apart and been just as close.

Jerry had been thinking about Gary lately so it didn't fully shock him when he saw Gary walking out of the new supermarket carrying a case of beer. Jerry hurriedly paid for his items, grabbed his little girl by the hand and ran out, reaching Gary just as he closed the trunk of his car. Gary recognized Jerry instantly. "Holy hell," he said.

"No kidding," said Jerry. "Can you believe we bump into each other here? And after all this time."

Gary looked at the bundle of diapers under Jerry's arm. "She looks a bit big for those," he said.

"No, not for her. We got a new one at home."

"With Patricia still?"

"Yep. Going strong. She'll flip when she hears I saw you."

"Be sure and tell her hello for me. She always was something else. Bev and I got divorced. Almost five years ago now."

They exchanged phone numbers and Gary told Jerry about a cabin his cousin had up in the mountains. The place was empty for the next couple of months and Gary thought Jerry might want to go for a weekend. "You know, catch up and have a laugh over the old days? Maybe do some fishing or something?" he'd said. Gary had never been to the cabin but his cousin had just that week offered him use of it. Gary knew nothing about fishing but this all sounded like a good idea. Jerry said he'd find out what weekend was best to leave Patricia with the kids. They drove out of the parking lot with smiles on their faces.

The next day Jerry called Gary to say that the weekend after this one coming would be good. "That work for you?" Jerry asked. "Absolutely," said Gary. "I'm free every weekend." Jerry was looking forward to the trip. He worried a lot about money and his job at the newspaper. He worried about his thinning hair vanishing by the hour.

Gary had forgotten about the trip until the Thursday before the Friday he was scheduled to pick up Jerry. Gary had once made an admirable attempt at being a responsible adult, but unable to be faithful to Bev and unable to keep a job for more than three months—and having spent a short time in prison for assault—he'd essentially reverted to being a high-schooler in his thirties, still wearing his long furry brown ponytail. He immediately went out shopping for supplies.

Gary hissed open two beers from a cooler in the back seat while Jerry hugged Patricia goodbye. The two old friends knocked their cans together as they pulled out of the driveway. It was about two hours up to the mountains. On the way they talked about life after school, people that they either didn't remember or had lost track of, and general events of the last few years. Later it became a quiet trip. Jerry, having dozed off, was waked by Gary's elbow and, "I think this is it." Gary's Chevy Cavalier handled a steep gravel path that ended at a small parking spot in an otherwise wooded area surrounding the cabin. "Take this," Gary said, handing Jerry a bloated duffle bag. Jerry took it and then grabbed his own bag and followed Gary, who had the large cooler by both hands, up to the cabin door. It was dark and cool out. Their crunchy gravel footsteps joined the sounds of insect nightlife. Gary left the car's headlights on so they could see their way into the house. He found a lantern, lit it with his Zippo, then made two more trips out to get the rest of his stuff. He turned the headlights off. "No power?" said Jerry. "Looks that way," said Gary, "but the cooler should last us the weekend. We'll cook the steaks tonight." There was a nearly full propane tank to heat the place and run the stove. Unsure of what to bring, Jerry had in his bag canned tuna, apples, bananas, bread, a gallon of water, and a bottle of wine. He looked at the supplies Gary had brought in and watched him unpack. Along with the steaks Gary had a whole chicken, eggs, milk, smoked salmon, coffee, bacon, spices, chocolate bars, peanut butter, beans, corn, tomatoes, rice, olive oil, cabbage, carrots, onions, potatoes, two cases of beer, six bottles of wine, a bottle of gin, and a bottle of port. "Are we sailing off to sea tomorrow?" Jerry said. "Help me get this fire going and I'll get dinner started. I'm starving," Gary answered.

The steaks were cooked just right, the fire was big, and after his second glass of wine Jerry fell asleep on the couch. Gary noted that this was the second time today he'd seen Jerry go to sleep. He finished his wine in front of the fire as he thumbed through Volume One of Ulysses S. Grant's memoirs, which he'd found on a bookcase by the window. When he started getting drowsy he gathered the steak bones and the rest of the garbage and took it out to a big metal trashcan behind the house. The bedroom had one bed and Gary left Jerry on the couch for the night. The supernatural silence on the mountain would normally have been unsettling, but after a little gin Gary had no trouble falling asleep. A few hours later he sprang up, startled by calamity. As his eyes tried to focus in the dark he heard nothing. He imagined he'd dreamt the commotion and fell back asleep.

In the morning Gary found Jerry frying eggs and drinking coffee. "Hey, thanks," he said. "No problem," said Jerry, "sleep ok?" "Yeah, you? I didn't want to bother you on the couch so I let you sleep. You take the bed tonight," said Gary. "Ah, don't worry about me," said Jerry. As they ate breakfast they talked about the possibility of going fishing. Was a lake or stream nearby? There was a shed behind the cabin and Gary said he'd go see if there were any fishing poles or equipment. He stepped outside, lit a cigarette, and walked towards the back of the cabin. When he rounded the corner he saw the trashcan dumped over, near empty and dented. "It was a goddamn bear!" Gary yelled. Jerry came out, "What?" "We've got a bear, man, look at this thing." Jerry looked at the mangled trashcan and said, "Are we in danger?" "I doubt it," said Gary, "but we ain't going fishing." They spent the afternoon drinking beer and playing cards. Jerry talked about his daughters, which he called his joys. Gary talked about how happy he was to be rid of Bev.

Gary later roasted the chicken with onions and potatoes, turning out another top-notch dinner. They stayed up late drinking port and Gary sensed that Jerry was fully enjoying himself. "Hey, if you want, I got something to take us back to the old days," said Gary. Holding what Jerry recognized as tabs of LSD, each with a tiny pentagram on it, Gary had his eyebrows raised and a wide grin on his face that showed his yellow teeth. "Whoa," said Jerry, "I've not seen that stuff in a long time. Where'd you get it?"

"Hey, I've got connections, baby."

"Lord, I think I'm too old for that."

"Come on, remember when Randy Meyers gave us acid at the prom? You had a great time!"

"I hardly remember our prom."

"Well, you had a great time. Trust me."

Gary was packing up the garbage when he had what he

thought was a brilliant idea. "If we have a bear," he said, "let's give it a treat." With a mischievous giggle Gary jammed several of the tabs of acid into the few edible pieces of trash before throwing the bag into the can out back. They played cards again for a while, reminding one another to listen for any noise. Later they stood at the back window, passing the bottle of port between them, whispering. Another hour passed. They were sitting in front of the fire drinking gin and discussing reincarnation when there was a knock at the door. "Did you hear that?" said Gary. "Someone's at the door," said Jerry. "It's three o'clock in the morning," said Gary, picking up the iron fireplace poker, "Who the hell's out here this time of night?" Jerry was standing behind the couch as Gary slowly opened the door. There was a rush of cold air. Backlit by the bright moon was the fully upright, near seven-foot-tall silhouette of a bear. Gary dropped the poker.

"Oh good, you're awake," said the bear. "I was afraid you might be sleeping but I saw light through the window. What're you doing?" There was silence for twenty seconds or so as the bear just stood in the doorway. "Uh, we—we were just talking about reincarnation," said Jerry. Ducking under the door frame and walking past Gary into the cabin the bear said, "Reincarnation? Would you believe in my previous life I was a race car driver?" The bear lifted the lid to the cooler and looked in. The bear pulled out a beer, drank it in nearly one gulp and then sat on the floor with a thump that shook the walls.

"Nice fire you've got going here boys."

"Uh, thanks. I'm Gary and he's Jerry."

"My name is Kirby."

"Hello Kirby," said Jerry.

"You guys really believe in that reincarnation stuff?"

"Well, I think it's possible," said Jerry, taking a seat by the fire next to Kirby, "but I don't believe in it."

"If you think it's possible, then you must believe in it."

"That's what I told him!" said Gary, joining them on the floor.

"Belief is the foundation of reality, no matter what your beliefs or your perceptions of reality are," said Kirby. "As Pascal said, 'Nothing fortifies skepticism more than that there are some who are not skeptics; if all were so, they would be wrong.' Got any more of these beers?"

"Do you shit the woods?" said Gary.

They all laughed.

"Was that salmon I saw you had in there, too?" said Kirby.

"Oh yeah," said Gary, "Are you hungry?"

"I'm a bear, I'm always hungry. Besides, you didn't leave much in the trash tonight."

Jerry got up and went to the cooler. He grabbed a beer, opened the smoked salmon and handed it to Kirby, "Help yourself."

The bear ate the entire package of fish in one giant paw-full. Jerry shivered slightly when he noticed how long and sharp Kirby's shiny black claws were.

"So, reincarnation," said Kirby, stabbing a claw through the top of his beer can. "In what form would you guys like to return to life?"

"I think I'd like to come back as a woman," said Gary with a laugh. "Maybe I could finally understand how their minds work."

"But would you then remember what it's like to be a man?" said Kirby. "You might have the same problem again, only in reverse, wanting to come back as a man someday, hoping to understand how *their* minds work. That could be endless."

Kirby turned to Jerry and said, "How about you, friend?"

"I don't know. What's it like being a bear? Maybe I could come back as a bear."

Laughter roared through Kirby's muscular jowls. The men could smell the bear's wild, rotten breath over the smoke of the fire. "Oh no, I'm not so sure you'd like it," the bear said still laughing, "You're probably better off coming back as a woman, too."

"Listen Kirby, it's late," said Jerry, "we should probably get some sleep."

"What? I thought you guys were cool. We've got a party happening here!"

"No, I'm tired," said Jerry, getting up off the floor.

"I don't think you understand," said Kirby, rising up on his back legs, "I'm not done here." His head almost touched the ceiling of the cabin. The bear flashed his massive yellow teeth as he swatted Jerry back to the ground with his heavy paw. The sound of Jerry's bones breaking echoed the crackle of the burning logs. Kirby mounted Jerry and began ripping at his sides. Gary jumped up and reached for the iron poker and started beating the bear across its back. The bear continued to ravage his friend. He positioned the iron rod in his hand like a javelin, and with all the strength in his body Gary thrust it into the spine of the bear. The bear let out a demonic howl and collapsed on top of Jerry. Gary blacked out.

When he regained consciousness, Gary found Jerry shredded and bloody lying on the floor in front of the couch. The fireplace poker was stuck deep into his chest. "Oh, God!" yelled Gary as he stood up. He paced next to Jerry's body, panting heavily. When he was able to slow down his breathing he began to talk to himself. "That bear must've survived. How? I bet he crawled out the door and died in front of the house. There's no other explanation. He couldn't have gotten far." The door was closed. Gary ran outside shouting "Kirby!" He saw nothing but trees and the parked car. "The bear is gone. That's not possible." He ran back inside and scanned the cabin. "There's no bear. There's no bear. This can't be happening." Gary went in the bedroom and got the quilt from the bed. With his foot on Jerry's neck he yanked the iron poker out through his ribs. He wrapped Jerry up in the quilt and carried him out to the shed behind the cabin. As Gary laid Jerry on the floor of the shed he noticed two fishing poles leaning against the wall. He latched up the shed and then started the Chevy. He backed down the gravel driveway in a panic, and drove off looking for Kirby.

RUSTY BUTLER AND THE TREMORS

It's an old story. Rusty Butler's girlfriend moved out. She felt their relationship was going nowhere, which meant she really felt that Rusty was going nowhere. They'd been together nearly two years and she threatened to break it off for good if Rusty didn't prove himself to be of some worth. She was a jealous girlfriend, though their relationship never warranted any jealousy. Rusty just always considered it part of her being a passionate person. He felt depressed without her. He knew he needed a life of his own but he also wanted Laurinne back. Lucky for Rusty, he might have a shot at both.

Laurinne's uncle owned a popular printing business. On several occasions he'd told Laurinne that Rusty could work for the company. Rusty had always dismissed the idea as pity from her family. Generosity and pity are two different things, Laurinne said. After two weeks spent alone in the house, Rusty decided to phone Uncle Theodore, who agreed to meet Rusty for a casual lunch.

In the living room wearing only his damp shower towel Rusty became anxious. He'd not had a haircut recently enough. Would they talk about Laurinne? Did Theodore know she'd moved out? What should he wear? What did Rusty know about printing that would make him valuable? A bounty of stress accompanied what should have been a simple hour out of Rusty's afternoon. Lighting a cigarette, Rusty sat on the couch, bent over the coffee table and turned on the TV. A few minutes later he caught himself staring at the floor. He got up and went into the bedroom to get dressed.

Years ago his father gave him a pinstripe Brooks Brothers shirt. Rusty only ever wore the shirt once and that was to his father's funeral. Searching for the pinstripe, he saw a shirt that he'd forgotten about. Laurinne, in an attempt to encourage job interviews last spring, had bought for him an expensive pale yellow Oxford shirt. Now was the time to put the shirt to work. Besides, Laurinne probably had better fashion sense than his dad. Their tiny closet was stuffed with cumbersome household items packed under the tight gathering of hanging clothes. There was an ironing board in there, a pair of crutches, a rolled up rug, an old lamp, a vacuum cleaner, some unusable curtain rods. The closet was built into the wall directly next to the bedroom window, which was cracked open nearly all year round. Rusty was wearing an undershirt, navy trousers, and his brown leather Bostonian shoes. He removed the yellow shirt from the hanger. Sliding his arms into the sleeves and reaching for the top button, he felt a sharp pinch in his left armpit, like a splinter going into his skin. His shoulders jerked with the pain and he threw the yellow shirt onto the bed. A fat female black widow spider ran from the collar, up the radiator and out the window. Rusty lifted his arm and saw two pink pin-hole dots on the soft flesh of his inner bicep. He put the shirt back on, tucked it in and greased his hair. The lunch meeting was scheduled for 1 p.m. at Novia Grasa. It was 12:38. He grabbed his coat and ran out to his car.

At a red light Rusty felt a cold sweat coming on and his underarm and chest were radiating a sinister warmth. He had a headache too and was feeling dizzy. After five more lights he was nauseous and the warmth in his chest had turned to a burn. St. Luke's Hospital wasn't far away, but he couldn't stand the thought of Uncle Theodore thinking he'd forgotten the meeting. Muscles in Rusty's back began to spasm and it was clearly unsafe to be driving. He made a right turn in the direction of the emergency room. By the time he got to the receptionist's desk he couldn't reach his back pocket to show identification because of the tremors in his arm. Rusty saw the nurse's face become a white light before he fainted on the waiting room floor.

His eyes opened and he was flat in a bed. Rusty looked at the clock on the wall and saw that it was nearly 4 p.m. A nurse walked by and he shouted for her. She came in and Rusty asked for his status. She told him that he'd been given antivenin for a spider bite and that he was going to be fine, he just needed rest. "La viuda negra," she whispered. When the nurse left, Rusty hopped out of bed and put on his clothes. He wobbled into the hallway, found a payphone, and dialed Laurinne's sister—he figured that's where she'd been staying. Running on the assumption that Laurinne was unaware of the appointment he'd scheduled with her uncle, he hoped to catch her before she spoke to Theodore and heard that he'd not shown. It was Laurinne that answered the phone and Rusty threw his head back with a smile of relief. He told her he met with Theodore and that he'd been offered a full-time job starting in three weeks. He invented a story about the meeting being brief because Theodore had to catch a plane to Mexico. Yeah, he was going to be away for close to a month and could not be reached until he returned. Laurinne sounded pleased with Rusty's initiative. He then called Theodore. No answer. He hung up the phone and walked out to his car.

Driving home, Rusty was coming back to life and was getting hungry. He found a parking spot right in front of his house and decided to walk the few more blocks to get some food. Arroz for Emily was run by a well-known family in town, and was as famous for being crowded as it was for its food. There were only five tables, and each sat just two guests. As Rusty was handed his lunch on a tray, an older couple got up from the table in the front window. He swooped in. A minute later, Rusty heard a voice from behind. He turned and saw a young woman holding a tray. She said she saw he had an extra seat and would he mind if she sat there. Rusty offered to share the table. She thanked him, sat down, and began eating. Rusty stared at her for a moment, watching her chew, then returned his attention to his own meal. They had the best table in the restaurant, up against the front window with the soon-to-be-set sun resting on their hands as they ate together in silence. When Rusty finished, he said have a nice evening to the girl and walked home.

The next morning Rusty made a pot of coffee and turned on the TV to the local news. He was to spend the afternoon cleaning the house. His plan was to scrub the bathroom, vacuum the carpet, wash the dishes in the sink, make the bed, and dust his bookshelf. He had decided to ask Laurinne to come for dinner. He looked through the refrigerator and the cupboards, trying to think what he'd cook. Despite having none of the ingredients, he felt like making meatballs. He would take a trip to the market after cleaning. Rusty refilled his coffee mug and went to the living room. There, standing at the open front door, was Laurinne. Her face was hot red and she was squeezing her purse with both hands. Her eyes were thin dashes and one side of her mouth was tightened up like she was gnawing on a toothpick.

"How dare you!" she said.

Rusty knew she'd spoken to her uncle.

"Who do you think you are? How dare you do this to me!"

Rusty started with, "Wait, listen," but it soon became clear it wasn't the missed meeting with Theodore that had her upset.

"Just because I'm not living here doesn't make you single!" She threw her purse at him, forcing his coffee to spill everywhere as he deflected the bag.

"What's wrong with you?" he shouted.

"I know what you've been doing." she said, stomping into the middle of the room.

"What? Doing what?" Rusty said.

"Donna saw you yesterday, don't even think about denying it."

Apparently Laurinne's friend Donna Rabia had passed by Arroz For Emily and seen Rusty in the front window dining with the stranger. Rusty said, "Oh, no, you don't understand," but Laurinne kept at it. As she continued to yell, Rusty suddenly chose not to defend his innocence. "I met her last week," he interrupted. "Her name is Araña and I'm in love with her. She's been sleeping here every night." Laurinne went silent. He looked to see what she could grab to throw at him.

"I never want to see you again!" she said, slamming the front door behind her. The couch was wet in spots from spilled coffee but he sat down. Rusty lit a cigarette and waited for the sound of Laurinne pulling away. Several minutes later he got up to fetch his car keys. He still felt like making meatballs.

On his way back from the market he passed a shop called Lehigh Exotic Pets. He pulled in. Rusty walked up to the man at the counter and asked if they had any black widow spiders. The man said they did have one for sale. As Rusty paid for the spider, the man warned him to be careful, listing the many necessary precautions. "Don't worry," Rusty said, "this isn't my first one." He brought the package home and set it on the living room floor. Removing the lid he peered into the plastic box. The big spider was motionless. He turned the box on its side, and with a gentle shake, the spider fell onto the carpet. It slowly crawled a few steps and then stopped. Rusty could see his face reflected in the spider's shiny, fat abdomen. He winked at himself and the black widow ran into the bedroom.

THIRD FLOOR, SECOND DOOR

I swear these walls are made of paper maché. They must be. These walls are so thin I'd bet they are hollow. Maybe stuffed in between with newsprint from the Great Depression for insulation. I wouldn't be surprised. This inhumanely small one-room apartment is like a display, like a diorama at a museum. Me, stuffed behind this wall with all my papers and junk piled to the ceiling, on exhibition, a superb example of the North American failure in its natural habitat.

My next door neighbor might as well just be my roommate. I can hear him roll over at night, talk on the phone, burp, fart, piss, and shit. He's old and miserable in every possible way. There is a large woman from another country who makes frequent visits over there. I've seen her standing outside his door through my two-way peephole that I keep obstructed with a cotton ball and a long vertical strip of tape. Whenever I hear footsteps or voices I push the cotton aside just enough to get a visual. She could very well be the result of some mail order program. Either way, the sounds that begin shortly after her arrival have the ability to control my mind in frightening ways. One night last summer when I was forced to hear all too well their hot relations, I began to march in circles in the middle of my room wearing only socks and my winter jacket, repeating the phrase, "Lord, have mercy on my soup." Also, the curmudgeon plays his spooky organ music at all hours of the night and day with the volume on his hi-fi so high that it vibrates my bookcase. I do not appreciate having my Keats rattled.

The young girl in the apartment on my other side, behind my bathroom mirror, is at times, more audible than the old coot. I'm rather certain that the layout of her apartment is mine in reverse. When I'm in my bathroom I can hear her brushing her teeth and doing all sorts of hair and face maintenance. I can even hear her exhale. It sounds as though her bathroom mirror, which no doubt also doubles as her medicine cabinet, is directly opposite mine. Often when I stare in the mirror I imagine her on the other side looking back at me. Only intimate couples use the bathroom together. I don't mind living with her. Partly because she's more pleasant in her overall ways than my other neighbor, but mostly because her proximity puts me physically closer than I've been to any woman in some time. I suppose I take comfort in knowing that a female is that near a part of my existence, and may possibly be as familiar with me as I am with her. One might, in a way, even consider us involved.

There are five small holes in the wall that joins my place with the old man's. I tell any rare visitors that these are bullet holes. In actuality the holes were made by the metal tip of my big pink golf umbrella. One Sunday afternoon the private concert I was unintentionally attending through the wall (which featured cellos harmonizing with hypnotic wails of erotic successes from the crotch master girlfriend) drove me to furiously attempt to spear clear into the center of hell. I wanted to stab my way right into his apartment and thrust my regal umbrella of a sword into the heart of the devil himself. I wanted to end his tyranny then and there as he lay naked under a heap of foreign flesh. The glory never came. All I ended up doing was jabbing five holes into my own wall. They never heard a thing. Of course, I could've knocked on his door, but that's not my style. I don't go out much.

The girl next door is, to me, exactly that, both in the literal sense and that of the popular phrase. She is young and looks clean and fresh and optimistic and motivated. I would wager she's not been living in the city long. She doesn't exactly seem the country mouse but she has certainly not yet been broken. I've attempted numerous times to catch her name by looking at her mail as she fetches it from her box but have had no luck. Nor have I yet found the courage or genuine need to borrow a cup of sugar or a shovel or a defibrillator or anything else that might have me standing casually at her open door. Our relationship has been strictly involuntary and by chance. Unless there is a Cupid of the real estate world, I am operating on my own fortune and will.

Wait. I'm going too fast. Let's start at simpler times. When I first moved in. Back when it was OK to drink in the afternoon. When you could tell the truth to your friends, no matter how small it could make them feel. Back to a time when space travel seemed irrelevant and smoking cigarettes was no big deal. This is when I began to come to life. The hatching of the great North American failure. My wobbling, uncertain infant head and my legs like that of a newborn colt, trembling and experimental. Ah, yes. It was an exciting time.

PATTERNS OF SIGNIFICANCE (I)

Lifting the blanket and slipping under the sheet as carefully as she could, she thought about who she'd least want to wake, Jim or the baby. Jim could be such an asshole when he woke up. Actually, so could the baby. The thought of her two-month-old baby being an asshole made her laugh out loud. She covered her mouth. She'd had a couple of drinks in front of the TV. She lay still. Her eyes stayed open. Well here I am, she thought, just me and a couple of assholes. She snorted a laugh then covered her mouth again. Jim rolled over. Rhinestones of sweat on his naked back twinkled in the moonlight. She reached and touched the pipe along the wall next to the bed. Christ, why is the heat on?

THEY BOTH GET THE STEW

What do you think about Toronto?

What about it?

I applied for a job there today.

It's in Canada.

Yes, I know.

It's cold there.

Not all the time.

Most of the time.

You've never been there.

Neither have you. Why did you apply for a job there?

Because I don't have one.

There're jobs here.

No, there aren't.

They speak French up there, you know.

They speak French in Quebec. Toronto is in Ontario.

What's the job?

Teaching English.

I thought they already spoke English.

Not teaching how to speak English. Books and papers and things.

You don't know about that stuff.

That's what I went to school for! You've never read a book in your life.

I have so.

What's your favorite book then?

A Tale of Two Cities.

OK, what two cities are in that book?

Smyrna and Toronto.

If I get this job we're moving to Canada.

We'd have to use different money.

Any money is different money for us.

That's the truth.

What are you getting?

I don't know. What do they eat in Toronto?

C'mon, let's order. I'm hungry.

Hey look at that guy in the corner. Doesn't he make movies?

What do you mean? He's *in* movies or he *makes* movies?

I mean what I said. He looks like that director, Ortiz.

He looks old to me.

Ortiz *is* old.

It must be him then.

Why is a famous movie director eating dinner all by himself?

Famous movie directors don't eat at this place. They don't regularly make it to Smyrna.

Should I go over?

Have you seen any of his movies?

I saw that one, about the cop that had the girlfriend with no legs.

I saw that. That's not one of his movies, is it?

Maybe not. It was good though. I wonder if Ortiz saw it.

Could we order please?

SO LIFELIKE

He had come in from mowing the lawn when we started going at it fast. He was on top of me from behind. His hand was pushed into the bed, near my face, as he supported himself pounding me. His hand smelled like gasoline. I imagined I was being raped in a garage. I came right then.

He was in the shower. I rolled over. I listened to the running water and wondered if this was just how it would always be. At least he was still attracted to me, I thought. Lots of married couples probably didn't have sex at all. And here it was three o'clock on a Sunday and I'd just come. Even if other wives were having sex with their husbands they were surely not having orgasms, I thought. I have no right to complain, I thought. But I still do. I can't help it.

I got dressed and walked out to the porch. In front of the house across the street the Hawkins kids played on the lawn. Miniature swimsuits, tiny inflatable pool, the hose, the sprinkler, the whole thing. I stood and watched the little Hawkinses scream and run in circles. Their laughter blew a breeze across our porch. A moment later the boy pushed the girl face down into the pool. She began to cry. Mrs. Hawkins appeared at the door. She picked up the wet girl and scolded the boy. She carried the girl inside and the boy followed.

I went back inside. The shower had stopped running. I went into the kitchen and poured some vodka into a glass of ice. I opened the refrigerator to get the orange juice when I heard the front door close. I walked over to the window in time to see him drive off. As I began to turn away I noticed something. At the end of our driveway, off to the side, there was a lump on the ground. I could see it was the doll the Hawkins girl often carried around. I walked down to the curb, bent over, and picked up the doll. I looked over at the Hawkins house. The house was silent.

Back in my kitchen I held the worn doll. It was made of cloth and had a brown skirt with white lace trim. I lifted the skirt and saw where its crotch was stitched. I straightened its tiny green sweater, brushed its yarn hair back, and ran my thumb over its flat, faded face. I stepped on the pedal that lifts the lid, threw the doll into the trash, and got the orange juice out of the fridge.

PATTERNS OF SIGNIFICANCE (II)

"Haven't you ever wondered what it would be like to kiss me?" she said. He thought going to a bar for lunch hadn't been the greatest idea. She'd had two whiskies with her soup. But he wanted to show his appreciation. It was her last day. Of course he'd imagined kissing her. Especially on the days when she wore the orange lip gloss. He was surprised she was leaning toward him with her hand on his leg. He was nearly twenty years older—and her boss. At least for a few more hours. Had she always seen him this way? Did it matter? Maybe she just wanted to hear him say she was pretty. "What's more boring than hearing someone talk about where they're from and what their life has been like?" she said. "You're here now. We're here and this is what's happening. Here and at this place and everywhere in the world. Isn't that enough? Who has time for anything else?" He watched her stab at the ice in her glass with the cocktail stirrer. He paid the bill then told her to go ahead and take the rest of the day for herself.

Walking instead of taking the bus, she wandered downtown and into her old neighborhood. Without really trying she was soon on her old block in front of her old building. It had been a long time. She'd lived alone there until she met Jim the asshole and moved in with him across the river. She looked up at her window. There were red curtains in there now. She walked over to her old favorite restaurant but it was now a different restaurant and it didn't look inviting. She walked a bit more then stopped in front of a hardware store. There was a TV in there. "Laverne & Shirley" was on. Were they lesbians? The day had worn off and it was dark. It got dark so early now. She looked down the street for the lights of any coming bus.

BLESSED ASSURANCE

So Gills was having a pretty good week so far. He slept at Elle's apartment last night after she bought him dinner and in the morning she reheated the chicken and he ate her pussy. He was walking home. The sun hurt his eyes. The city was bright orange and he had trouble seeing where he was going but he didn't want it to end. It was cold out, but a nice sharp cold. As he turned onto his street the sunlight gave way to definite reds and whites. The street was blocked with vehicles and people. His building was on fire. He crossed over to his building only to be told, you can't go in there. Gills looked up and saw his window framed in charcoal. He touched his pockets. All he had on him was all he had. In front of his building had always stood a four-foot or so white marble statue of the Virgin Mary. He looked carefully to make sure she was still untouched. He walked the twelve or so blocks back to Elle's apartment but she'd left for the day for work.

Gills went to a diner to take inventory. He had enough money for eggs, toast, and coffee but no more. Coffee refills were free. In his coat he had a pocketknife, a small notebook, a stubby pencil, a subway token, and Elle's lipstick. He wished he had a cigarette. He didn't dwell on losing his apartment. He hated that apartment—and his landlord. He hadn't paid rent for the last two months. He wasn't sad over the belongings he'd lost, but he did care about several books he'd read several times. At least the public library was still standing. His bed and desk and chair had come with the apartment. He smirked when he remembered a girl once saying he ought to burn his dirty sheets and blankets. There were some photographs in the desk drawer he knew would now be gone. He'd looked at those enough anyway. Eating as slowly as he could, he stared out the window and tried to remember where Elle worked.

Elle worked as a travel agent. This morning she was working on getting an older couple to Canada. They'd never been out of the United States and this trip was a big deal. The trouble Elle was having was, that for the couple, air travel was too expensive and ground transportation took too long. Elle wanted to yell at them, "Either you want to go or you don't!" They were indecisive and seemingly uninterested in something that was meant to be exciting, or interesting at the least. Elle wondered how the two had made it this far along in life, much less together. It was exhausting trying to get people places they said they wanted to go when they continuously resisted.

Elle got an early break for lunch, only after getting the elderly pair to consider the airfare. She bought a tuna salad sandwich with too much pickle relish in it and sat on a park bench to eat. As she started for the second half of her sandwich a man sat on the bench next to her. She looked at him and saw he had sores on his hands. His hair was long and his beard didn't much hide his chapped burnt skin. She looked at her sandwich and then asked the man if he was hungry. He said no but thanked her. She looked at his clothes, thin and dirty. It was a sharp cold outside and she knew he must be cold. "Would you take my scarf and hat?" she asked. He lifted his head to look at her for the first time in her eyes. She watched his eyes move to the thick plaid wool scarf on her neck and then to the white knit hat on her head. He said, "You need those more than I do." Elle took off her scarf and wrapped it around the man's neck, nearly hugging him. She pulled her hat down over his greasy hair. "I have more than I need," she said with a smile, getting up to walk away, leaving the untouched other half of the sandwich wrapped on the bench. As she crossed the street she thought she heard the man say, "Bitch."

After a few hours at the diner, Gills decided to walk back to his block. The flames had died down but the commotion had not. People crowded the sidewalk and fire hoses lay across the road as water dripped from the building to mix with ash on the street. Gills asked a fireman if anyone was allowed in the building and the tired fireman said, "I'm afraid not, son." Gills pointed to the charred window frame and told the man that that was his apartment up on the third floor. The fireman said that he was sorry and that everything was gone, then said, "Excuse me but I'm needed," and walked away, turning around to say once again that he was sorry.

Gills went over to the little statue of the Virgin Mary. She was still shining, not a smear of ash on her. He found Elle's lipstick in his pocket. He took it out and extended the gentle red part fully. He put the tip to the Virgin Mary's white mouth and rubbed the bright color onto her lips. He stepped back then moved in and pressed his lips to hers for a long time hard. Gills then walked away without looking back. He licked his lower lip and thought about praying for snow.

ST. MATTHEW'S FINGER, ST. PETER'S THUMB

I have the bedroom window open in July in my apartment in Venice. There is no screen. I have Diana on her back on the bed. There is no breeze. We're high up enough that no neighbors get a show, but we're not so high up that—I'd like to add at this point that we've gone this afternoon to the "Tintoretto Church" in Cannaregio, the Madonna something-or-other, and seen three or so of Tintoretto's paintings, and his tomb with his family down in there, too. I don't mean to be gawky or make a spectacle of his work and death and stuff, but it was a big deal. Later in the afternoon at the San Rocco place with his paintings on the ceiling, up on the top floor, unopened until now for a century, I saw some old bones, preserved fingers, the ecclesiastical digits of holy men in vases.

Anyway, so I'm fucking Diana when the unmistakable

flap of a pigeon sounds behind me. I'm kind of busy and don't think much of it until I hear the bird make that stupid coo they do like a drunken owl and I know it's closer than I'd like. I pull out and turn my head and there it is on the sill, not but three feet from my feet, poised to join us in the room. "Whoorld," it coos. "Don't stop," Diana groans. I pop back in and hope the dove of shame doesn't charge at my ass with its claws. The bird is silent as Diana comes. I keep pushing and then it's my turn to tingle. Just as I'm getting to the good part I hear the pigeon flap again and lift off. I feel it shit on my back as it coasts over us. I then see it land at the top of my bookcase. I keep on and come big inside Diana. It's quiet for a moment as I collapse. Once I regain regular breathing, I say, "Shit." Diana says, "What?"

"There's shit on my back," I say, "that fucking bird."

"What fucking bird?" she says.

"That fucking bird up there!" I say, pointing to the bookcase.

"Jesus."

"Fucker shit on my back."

After another quiet moment, Diana says, "Did it feel good?"

"No!" I say, "I have to wipe that shit off."

"Not that!" she says. "When you did it inside me."

"Oh, yes," I say, "it felt so good."

"It felt good for me, too," she says.

She kisses my forehead then gets up and goes into the bathroom. I get up and go to the bookcase. The bird has been perched since I came. With a few waves of a lit cigarette the pigeon wobbles and puffs then flaps its way over the empty bed and out the window. I look closer at the top shelf. The bird has also shit on my books. It's covered an impressive range, soiling Beckett, Berryman, Bishop, Bronte, and Browning. I need to get this shit off my back. Diana comes from the bathroom and hands me a towel. I wipe off the books first.

PATTERNS OF SIGNIFICANCE (III)

She slid out of bed, put on Jim's sneakers and went onto their little terrace. She'd forgotten to turn off the multi-colored Christmas tree lights that were threaded through the iron railing. She took the lid off a cookie jar and got the pack of cigarettes she kept in there. Smoking in the clear night she heard the sad Greek music coming from her downstairs neighbor's radio. It was as loud as usual but it was never on this late. Her downstairs neighbor was ninety-three, nearly deaf, and lived alone. Her first thought was that maybe he'd died with the radio on. Maybe he'd died looking at pictures of him and his dead wife filled with a young love. Maybe he'd never loved her at all. Maybe there'd never been anyone. Maybe it was just him and that radio for decades. She put out her cigarette in a plant and went back to bed, considering again who she might disturb.

WE WERE ALL FISH ONCE

Almost from the start we've been calling him Ed. Ever since we found out he was coming. Even before we knew he was a he, Ed was the name.

Diana teaches math at the junior high school so she has most of the summer off. The school year ended when she was about four months pregnant so she's bigger now that we're into August. It's our first kid and saying we're excited doesn't cover it. We tried for some time before Ed proved to be the fighter he is. We can now feel and see him kicking and punching and flipping around inside Diana.

Diana was on the couch with a TV tray set up in front of her in front of the TV. The news was on as I finished up a big batch of red beans and rice. I always use andouille sausage and never skimp on the Old Bay. Garnish with Saltines and a bottle of hot sauce.

After dinner and the dishes were done we were watching

"CHiPs" and talking about what Ed was going to look like. What color eyes would he have? Brown like hers or hazel like mine? Could he have blues eyes? We didn't know. Would he be born bald like I was or with a tuft of black hair like Diana was? Whose nose would he have?

I said to Diana that maybe we should take a look and see how he's coming along. You know, answer some questions. How would we do it, she asked. I looked around the living room and then pointed to the fish tank. We could use that, I said. You think so, she asked. Sure, I said, here. I got up off the couch and filled a big mixing bowl from the kitchen full of water from the sink. I got the netted utensil for the tank and scooped out our two big fat goldfish and plopped them into the bowl. I set the bowl on the kitchen counter. The fish were fine. I turned off the TV and set the TV tray off to the side. I told Diana to pull down her underwear from under her skirt and put her feet up on the coffee table with her legs apart. I crawled up under and in between Diana's legs and looked up at her vagina. You can do this, she said. I put my hands together in prayer fashion and pushed my fingers and thumbs up into Diana.

Ed was still small at six months and I felt I had him all in my hands all at once. But I knew it was more tricky. He was slippery and his head was way bigger than everything else. Diana groaned with discomfort. I pulled toward myself with both hands on what I thought was his butt. My fingertips cradled the whole lump and everything came forward. Out slid Ed. Diana didn't scream, but made more of a shocked gulp noise. I immediately tossed Ed into the fish tank. I was afraid he might try to breathe air. Not yet, son.

I panicked slightly when Diana sprang up and said, Do you have the cord? I said, No, do you? She said, It's here, I see it on the floor but don't let it get dirty. I grabbed a clean towel and rested the slim umbilical cord on the floor. I never imagined it would be so long. Diana collapsed back with a sigh of exhaustion. She was sweating. I pushed aside her bangs and blew on her forehead and neck. Her heartbeat slowed to normal and I sat next to her on the couch. We hugged and then looked together at the tank. Ed was curled up with his eyes closed. It was too early to see what color they would be. There wasn't much for hair anywhere but I could tell he was going to have Diana's nose. His little fingers were balled into fists and his tiny toes were so precious. We could see his first toenails already. He would roll sometimes in the tank. I imagined an alligator in a bathtub. Ed was graceful though, each movement calculated, and peaceful. That's my boy, I thought. No wonder it's called the fetal position. Ed was surely tucked into himself.

Diana and I must've sat there for an hour admiring Ed with all our love. So proud of what we'd done. We knew we had a long way to go but he was so beautiful already. Once the magic dimmed I said to Diana, How do we get him back in? Diana said, It ought to be easy, just line his feet up then push him in from his shoulders; he should slide right in. What if he doesn't want to go back in, I asked; I mean, we were all fish once. He'll go right back, Diana said, he's got plenty of time. I guess you're right, I said, as I tried to visualize thrusting my boy back into his mom's pussy by his brittle shoulders and collarbones. Maybe we should look at him a little more, Diana said. I was relieved she'd bought me more time before having to send Ed back, but truly too I knew that this was something we'd always remember. I looked to see that the cord was still connected and cleanly resting on the towel. I put my arm around Diana and let out a sigh. Then I suddenly remembered the fish.

Robert Overbey is a writer of mostly short fiction. He was a shortlist finalist for the Faulkner Society's Pirate's Alley writing competition and a shortlist finalist for the Paris Lit Up short story prize. His work has appeared in *Sakura Review* and he is a regular contributor to *Alexandria Quarterly*. He received a BFA in creative writing from Goddard College. He lives in New York City.

A version of "Pedderson's Uncle" appeared in *Sakura Review*. Versions of "Don't Forget the Dill," "We Were All Fish Once," "Venus Spins the Other Way," "Bullseye," "So Lifelike," "Born Together," and "Blessed Assurance" appeared in *Alexandria Quarterly*.

Made in the USA
Charleston, SC
26 July 2016